The R
art. They built
house

D0015864

DATE DUE

libraries

MAY 0 5 2011	
JUL 1 9 2012	
APR 1 8 2015	

ness
nters.

Empe
eight

k

The w
as gro
many,

en
of
s.

GAYLORD   PRINTED IN U.S.A.

Regarding the Bathrooms

Other books written by Kate Klise
and illustrated by M. Sarah Klise:

Regarding the Fountain
Regarding the Sink
Regarding the Trees
Letters from Camp
Trial by Journal
Shall I Knit You a Hat?
Why Do You Cry?

Also by Kate Klise:

Deliver Us From Normal

Regarding the Bathrooms

A Privy to the Past

Kate Klise

Illustrated by M. Sarah Klise

Harcourt, Inc.

Orlando Austin New York San Diego Toronto London

Epigraph by Ani DiFranco taken from an interview
published in *Eye Weekly,* March 1995.

www.HarcourtBooks.com

Library of Congress Cataloging-in-Publication Data
Klise, Kate.
Regarding the bathrooms: a privy to the past/by Kate Klise; illustrated by M. Sarah Klise.
p. cm. — (Regarding the—)
Summary: In this novel told through letters, newspaper articles,
and police reports, a middle school principal's bathroom renovation project
leads to the discovery of stolen Roman antiquities.
[1. Middle schools—Fiction. 2. Schools—Fiction. 3. Mystery and detective stories.
4. Humorous stories.] I. Title: Privy to the past. II. Klise, M. Sarah, ill. III. Title. IV. Series.
PZ7.K684Rc 2006
[Fic]—dc22 2005016813
ISBN-13: 978-0-15-205164-8 ISBN-10: 0-15-205164-3

Designed by M. Sarah Klise with assistance from Barry Age and Matthew Willis

First edition
C E G H F D

Printed in the United States of America

This is a work of fiction. All the characters in this book are the product of the author's
and the illustrator's *plumb crazy* imaginations. But this much is true: Reading, like bathing,
is restorative. The creators of this book suggest you enjoy this story while taking a bath—
or simply relaxing in the bathroom. And if anyone disturbs you, tell them to call us!

For *Eliza von Zerneck*—
May you always be young and silly enough
to enjoy a *loo*dricous story like this.

"I'd rather be able to face myself in the bathroom mirror than be rich and famous."

Ani DiFranco

GEYSER CREEK MIDDLE SCHOOL
From the Principal's Desk
Labor omnia vincit.
(Work conquers all.)

Mr. Walter Russ
Principal

June 14

Florence Waters
President
Flowing Waters Fountains, Etc.
Watertown, California

Dear Ms. Waters,

Thank you for agreeing to help me prepare for the upcoming Society of Principals and Administrators (SPA) conference in Geyser Creek.

As you know, SPA is the official organization for school principals, like me, and administrators. Every year we meet to discuss new trends in school management.

As host of this year's SPA conference, I am responsible for giving a speech about my management philosophy, *Labor omnia vincit.* (That's Latin for "Work conquers all.") I will then lead the principals and administrators on a tour of our school, culminating in a banquet at Cafe Florence.

My biggest concern—besides the speech, which I have not yet started—is the condition of the bathrooms in the school basement. I cringe when I think of 300 principals from around the country seeing our filthy basement lavatories, especially the graffiti covering the bathroom walls.

I realize, Ms. Waters, that a bathroom renovation is a far cry from the exciting projects you've helped us with in the past. (I refer to your work regarding the fountain, regarding the sink, and most recently regarding the trees on our school campus.)

But please remember that the purpose of middle school is not to provide excitement but to instill in students a lifelong love of reading, writing, arithmetic—and a healthy respect for clean restrooms.

The SPA conference is August 31. Attached is a work order.

Sincerely,

Walter Russ

GEYSER CREEK MIDDLE SCHOOL

WORK ORDER

PROJECT: Renovation of the basement bathrooms

DEADLINE: August 31

AUTHORIZED BY: (WR)

PHOTOS OF PROJECT:

GIRLS

BOYS

SPECIAL INSTRUCTIONS:

The bathrooms should be renovated in a traditional design. Something classic would be good.

(Pardon my sloppy handwriting. I'm under a lot of stress these days.)

Watertown, California

OVERNIGHT EXPRESS

June 16

Wally Russ
Princey Pal
Geyser Creek Middle School
Geyser Creek, Missouri

Dear Wally,

You and your work orders! Haven't you learned by now that ordering people around doesn't *work*?

Never mind. I *adore* traditional bathrooms and will consider helping you renovate the school's basement bathrooms in a classic style—*if* you promise to never again send me one of those dreadful work orders. (Poo on work!)

There. I'm glad that's settled. I leave for vacation next week.

Toodles! *Florence*

P.S. Where are you spending your summer vacation, Wally? May I suggest a trip to a spa? It would do wonders to relieve your stress.

From the Principal's Desk
Labor omnia vincit.
(Work conquers all.)

Mr. Walter Russ
Principal

June 17

Florence Waters
President
Flowing Waters Fountains, Etc.
Watertown, California

Dear Ms. Waters,

I hardly have time for a vacation with the SPA conference right around the corner.

Perhaps I wasn't clear. Three *hundred* principals and school administrators from across the country will be coming to Geyser Creek Middle School for this conference. High-ranking SPA officials will also be in attendance.

I hope you can understand why this is so stressful for me, and why I am eager for your help.

I won't send you any more work orders if you'll please just renovate our basement bathrooms in a traditional style. Also, there must be no evidence of waste in the project.

Efficiently yours,

Walter Russ

Walter Russ

P.S. The only travel plans I have this summer are trips to the bathroom.

FLOWING WATERS FOUNTAINS, ETC.

Watertown, California

June 20

Wally Russ
Principal & Recovering Know-It-All
Geyser Creek Middle School
Geyser Creek, Missouri

Dear Wally,

Really? Me, too! I'm leaving right now on a trip to my Bath room. Write to me at:

> 4 Bubble Street
> Bath, England

I'll think about your restroom renovation there. Don't we all do our best thinking in a well-appointed Bath room?

I'm assuming your students will assist me in this renovation. I'd be plumb crazy to plunge into a project this serious (*hee-hee*) without consulting my favorite pen pals. They're always flush with great ideas!

Cheerio, Wally-o! *Florence*

P.S. Don't worry about the visiting principals seeing evidence of waste. The simplest flushing mechanism will take care of that.

P.P.S. Please don't fret about the SPA conference. Everyone will be charmed by your lovely school and town. Nothing bad *ever* happens in Geyser Creek!

((◀ ALL POINTS BULLETIN ◀))

Geyser Creek
County
Sheriff's Office

Date: June 21   **Time:** 0805

Sheriff Mack Rell here reporting a breakout at the
Geyser Creek County Jail. Escaped cons on the loose.
Yep, it's those two again: Sally Mander and Dee Eel,
the downest, dirtiest, meanest-dealing duo this town
has ever known.

All officers are expected on duty ASAP.

Well, since it's just you and me, Sting, I guess
I'll see you when you get here, okeydokey?

Can you pick up some of Angel's glazed donuts on
your way? Thanks and bye-bye. I mean, over and out.

☆ THE GEYSER CREEK GAZETTE ☆
Our motto: "We have a nose for news!"

| Tuesday, June 21 | Late Edition | 50 cents |

Sally Mander and Delbert "Dee" Eel Escape!
Town's most famous villains on the loose

A search is under way for Sally Mander and Delbert "Dee" Eel. The duo escaped from the Geyser Creek County Jail sometime after 10 p.m.

Little information is available about the breakout.

"I checked on 'em last night," said Geyser Creek Sheriff Mack Rell. "They were both in their cells. But when I went over this morning to take Sal and Dee their breakfasts, they were gone."

Sally Mander   Dee Eel

The side-by-side cells showed no signs of having been tampered with, and the locks were still intact. The only clue, said Rell, is a note found in Mander's cell. (See photo below.)

Rell assigned Lieut. Sting Ray to lead the search for the missing inmates.

Thirteen months ago, Mander and Eel were found guilty of fraud, misrepresentation, greed, weasel-like conduct and slimy business practices for their role in capping off a geyser underneath Geyser Creek Middle School.

The duo redirected the water to the Dry Creek Swimming Pool and Dry Creek Water Company, owned by Mander and Eel, respectively. They were each sentenced to 30 years without the possibility of parole. Before her conviction, Sally Mander also served as president of the local school board.

"Sally and Dee built the middle school 31 years ago on the cheap and the quick," said Lily, a student at Geyser Creek Middle School. "They were so greedy to cap off the geyser, they didn't

even bother to build a gym or a library in the middle school."

"And Sally made kids pay extra to swim at her pool," added classmate Paddy. "What a meanie."

Lily and Paddy worked with fellow classmates at Geyser Creek Middle School last year to uncover Mander and Eel's crimes.

"Fortunately, we're all signed up for summer school," said Lily. "Just in time to help with this new development!"

Sally Mander's Parting Message

My sister, Liz Ard, had nothing to do with this.
-Sally Mander

This note was found in a sealed envelope in Sally Mander's jail cell.

Principal Russ to Host SPA Conference

Principal stressed out about cons and johns.

Geyser Creek Middle School Principal Walter Russ will host the upcoming conference of the Society of Principals and Administrators (SPA).

(Continued on page 2, column 2)

First Day of Summer Tradition Continues

Locals turn out to see sun rise between boulders.

Call it our local "sunrise special."

The sun rose this morning, the first day of summer, between two boulders at the east entrance to the old Dry Creek Swimming Pool.

"Did y'all see that?" asked hairstylist Pearl O. Ster, one of several locals who have made getting up early to watch the summer solstice sunrise an annual tradition. "It's just so ding-dang pretty."

No one can explain how or why the sun rises exactly between the two giant boulders every year on the first day of summer. When asked about it before her imprisonment and subsequent escape, former pool owner Sally Mander said, "How's it work? How the heck should I know? Those stupid boulders were there when I bought this old dump."

Similar boulders are located throughout Geyser Creek.

Did y'all know?

The word *solstice* is Latin for "sun stands still." *Solstice* comes from the Latin words *sol* (sun) and *stasis* (to stand still).

Rome, Paris ... Geyser Creek?
"Why not?" asks Mayor I. B. Newt

Mayor Newt convenes tourism task force.

With a geyser, a geyser-fed creek and the beautiful Jawlseedat Mountain just a stone's throw away, you'd think Geyser Creek would be a popular tourist destination.

Think again.

"Nobody comes to Geyser Creek for vacation anymore," lamented Geyser Creek Mayor I. B. Newt at last night's city council meeting.

Although it was a popular tourist destination in generations past, Geyser Creek no longer attracts summer vacationers.

"We need to give people a reason to visit," said Newt.

Unable to think of a reason, the mayor issued a special proclamation and convened a tourism task force to explore ways to attract tourists to Geyser Creek and the Jawlseedat Mountain region.

PRINCIPAL *(Continued from page 1, column 2)*

Russ stated that until this morning, his biggest challenge was getting the school's basement bathrooms in presentable condition before the conference on August 31. He has asked designer Florence Waters to oversee the project.

"Now, of course, I'm more stressed out about having escaped convicts on the loose," Russ ruminated.

Russ will have to worry about the cons and the johns—and write his own letters to Ms. Waters—without the help of school secretary Goldie Fisch-N., who is taking the summer off for personal reasons.

Welcome to summer school!

What shall we study this summer? How about geology?

Today's geological fact: Most geysers are located in areas of high volcanic activity.

Too boring!!! It's summer. Let's study fun things!

movies *recess* *magic tricks*

Anything but WORD OF THE DAY!

Okay.

TODAY'S ASSIGNMENT: Find somewhere to volunteer this summer.

Summer volunteer projects:
    Mr. N.: Planting a garden behind school.

Please be careful when walking to/from school!

WANTED

Sally Mander

Delbert "Dee" Eel

Congratulations on your wedding, Mr. N.!

Postcards from Florence

June 22

Ms. Annette Trap
Editor, *The Geyser Creek Gazette*
On the Square
Geyser Creek, Missouri

Dear Ms. Trap,

Do you by any chance need an investigative reporter?

I don't know much about journalism, but I've been writing letters to Florence Waters for two years, and I'm pretty good at that.

Please think about it and let me know.

Thanks!

Tad Poll

P.S. You don't have to pay me. I want to volunteer.

SUMMER IS COOL
(even if you're in summer school)

Geyser Creek Middle School
Geyser Creek, Missouri

June 22

Mayor I. B. Newt
Geyser Creek City Hall
On the Square
Geyser Creek, Missouri

Dear Mayor Newt,

I think Geyser Creek has a lot to offer. I'd love to help you think of ways to attract visitors to this area.

Let me know if you're interested. I'd be happy to volunteer as your summer intern.

Sincerely,

Shelly

SUMMER IS COOL
(even if you're in summer school)

Geyser Creek Middle School
Geyser Creek, Missouri

June 22

Ms. Jeannie Ologee
Director, Geyser Creek His, Hers, and Theirs-torical Society
206 Second Street
Geyser Creek, Missouri

Dear Ms. Ologee,

Could you use some help this summer? If so, I'd like to volunteer.
As you know, I really like studying history and <u>herstory</u>.

Your friend and (I hope) summer assistant,

Minnie O.

SUMMER IS COOL
(even if you're in summer school)

Geyser Creek Middle School
Geyser Creek, Missouri

June 22

Mr. Walter Russ
Principal
Geyser Creek Middle School
Geyser Creek, Missouri

Dear Principal Russ,

I'm writing to apply to be your summer volunteer administrative assistant. If you choose me for the job, I'll do my very best. I'll even help you write letters to Florence Waters.

If you don't pick me for the job, that's okay. I'm sure there are other people who are better qualified. But I hope you'll give me a chance. I've never had a real job before.

Sincerely,

Gil

SUMMER IS COOL
(even if you're in summer school)

Geyser Creek Middle School
Geyser Creek, Missouri

June 22

Sheriff Mack Rell
Geyser Creek County Sheriff's Office
Geyser Creek, Missouri

Dear Sheriff Mack Rell,

We would like to help you catch Sally Mander and Delbert "Dee" Eel.

As you recall, it was our class that uncovered Ms. Mander and Mr. Eel's slimy business dealings last year.

Even though we're young, we're experienced and highly motivated investigators.

Let us know how we can help. We can begin work TODAY!

Your partners in crime solving,
Lily   Paddy

P.S. If you need a reference, please contact Florence Waters.

DATE TODAY HOUR NOW
TO Mr. N.

WHILE YOU WERE OUT

M GARDENING
OF
PHONE

❑ Telephoned ❑ Returned Call ❑ Left Package
❑ Please Call ❑ Was In ❑ Please See Me
❑ Will Call Again ❑ Won't Call ❑ Important

MESSAGE: YOUR SUMMER SCHOOL MAILBOX IS FULL. PLEASE COME PICK UP LETTERS TO YOUR CLASS.

Signed Walter Russ

✫ THE GEYSER CREEK GAZETTE ✫

"We have a nose for news!"

Annette Trap, Editor

June 23

Tad Poll
c/o Geyser Creek Summer School
Geyser Creek Middle School
Geyser Creek, Missouri

Dear Tad,

I'm always looking for good reporters!

Come over to the paper tomorrow. You can help me put the paper to bed. (That's the expression we use to describe finishing an edition of the paper.)

Don't worry about your lack of experience. The only thing you really need to know about journalism is the concept of the inverted triangle:

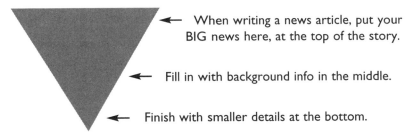

← When writing a news article, put your BIG news here, at the top of the story.

← Fill in with background info in the middle.

← Finish with smaller details at the bottom.

We lay out the newspaper in the same way, with the biggest news story at the top of the front page. Smaller, less significant stories are buried inside.

I'll tell you the rest when you get here. This'll be fun!

A. Trap

Annette Trap

OFFICIAL PROCLAMATION

HIS HONOR
MAYOR I. B. NEWT

WHEREAS, Shelly has volunteered to be my summer intern, and

WHEREAS, heck knows I could use some help running this town, and

WHEREAS, Shelly's willing to work for free . . .

I hereby appoint

SHELLY

to the office of
Summer Intern to the Mayor!

And I declare that in said capacity
she shall attend the next meeting
of my Tourism Task Force,
which is scheduled for . . .

Hmmm... Looks like that meeting hasn't been scheduled yet. Okay, kiddo, your first task as my summer intern is to schedule the meeting, let everyone know when it is, and plan the agenda.

Signed on this day,
June 23

I.B. Newt

Mayor of Geyser Creek, Missouri

June 23

Minnie O.
Summer School
Geyser Creek Middle School
Geyser Creek, Missouri

Dear Minnie,

I'd love a summer assistant!

Thanks to you and your classmates, we've put together a good history of our town over the past 100 years. But I can't help wondering what Geyser Creek was like 500 years ago—or even a thousand years ago. Who settled this area, and why did they come here? There's nothing in the archives about this.

As my summer assistant, please research the ancient history of Geyser Creek and the entire Jawlseedat Mountain area. It's his-, her-, and *our*story.

Sincerely,

Jeannie Ologee

Jeannie Ologee

GEYSER CREEK MIDDLE SCHOOL
From the Principal's Desk
Labor omnia vincit.
(Work conquers all.)

Mr. Walter Russ
Principal

June 23

Gil
c/o Mr. N.'s Summer School Class
Geyser Creek Middle School
Geyser Creek, Missouri

Gil,

Because yours was the only application I received,
you have the job. Congratulations.

Your first task as my administrative assistant is to write
to Florence Waters for an update on the bathroom
renovation project. You'll find Ms. Waters in her Bath
room. The address is on my desk.

After that you can begin writing my speech for the
SPA conference. The topic is my management
philosophy: Work conquers all. I'll expect to see a first
draft by lunchtime.

Keep working.

Walter Russ

June 23

Lily and Paddy
Geyser Creek Middle School
Summer School
Geyser Creek, Missouri

Dear Lily and Paddy,

Thanks for your letter, girls. It was real sweet. But the rules don't allow me to use volunteer investigators—especially when they're only 12 years old.

Don't worry. I've got Sting Ray working all the angles. He knows this case backward and forward. Remember, he's the one who searched Sally's and Dee's offices last year and found all those ~~innsrimminn~~ ~~incrumminatty~~ nasty letters and faxes and stuff.

If you want to help, how 'bout investigating what's going on over at Geyser Creek Cafe? Has Angel moved? I miss those glazed donuts.

Mack Rell

Mack Rell

SUMMER IS COOL
(even if you're in summer school)

Geyser Creek Middle School
Geyser Creek, Missouri

Hand Delivered

June 24

Sheriff Mack Rell
Geyser Creek County Sheriff's Office
Geyser Creek, Missouri

Sheriff Mack Rell,

Herewith our report on the Case of the Missing Glazed Donuts:

The facts: Angel Fish closed her cafe so she and her husband, aka* Chef Angelo, could open Cafe Florence. The grand opening is today.

But don't count on any donuts, glazed or otherwise. Our sources tell us that Angel let Chef Angelo place the food order for the summer. Chef Angelo moved to Geyser Creek from Italy just three months ago, so his English is not so great. He flubbed up the order and bought 1,000 pounds of chicken, 200 dozen eggs, and

---

*aka stands for "also known as."

22

5,000 pounds of chocolate. That and a few spices are all they have to cook with this summer.

Angel is allegedly furious because now they don't have enough money to buy the ingredients she needs to make her famous glazed donuts.

This concludes our report.

Your deputies in training (please?),

Lily   Paddy

P.S. We'd start the Mander and Eel investigation by talking to Sally Mander's only sister, Liz Ard. As you know, Liz was our town historian. Last year when we were working on our town history report, we asked for her help. She refused, saying she'd lost all of the town's old records. Fat chance. With your permission, we'd like to ask Liz Ard what really happened to those historical documents, and what in the world Sally Mander meant in that note she left behind in her jail cell. (It looks a little suspicious to us.)

June 24

Lily and Paddy
Geyser Creek Middle School
Summer School
Geyser Creek, Missouri

Dear Lily and Paddy,

Dang-it-all, girls. I'm sorry, but this is a
serious case. If you really want to help, how
about just staying out of the way, okay?

Mack Rell

Mack Rell

P.S. I told Sting your ideas about Liz Ard. He
said he knows all about it. He's leaving right
now to ~~interryrgait~~ ~~intearigate~~ talk to her.

INTERROGATION OF LIZ ARD
BY LIEUT. STING RAY

TRANSCRIPT

Sting Ray: Okay, Liz, where are those historical documents you supposedly lost?

Liz Ard: I don't know.

Sting Ray: Cut the cute stuff, Ard. You're looking at jail time for obstruction of justice.

Liz Ard: You're serious?

Sting Ray: As a heart attack.

Liz Ard: All right, all right. I'll talk. I was town historian for 40 years. I took pride in my job, visiting the local schools, talking to children about our town's history.

Sting Ray: Yada-yada-yada. Get to the point, Liz. Something happened when you were town historian. What was it?

Liz Ard: Okay, I'll tell you. I found something 32 years ago in the city archives.

Sting Ray: What?

Liz Ard: A map.

Sting Ray: Big deal.

Liz Ard: You don't understand. This was a map to the most valuable thing on Earth: the Fountain of Youth!

Sting Ray: A magical spring with the power of eternal youth. Anyone who bathes in it or drinks from it will never grow old.

Liz Ard: Exactly.

Sting Ray: It doesn't take a rocket scientist to see you didn't find it, Liz. Those liver spots are a dead giveaway.

Liz Ard: You're cold, Sting.

Sting Ray: I'm an investigator first and a gentleman second.

Liz Ard: Okay, so I didn't find the Fountain of Youth. But I found the map to it. And it was authentic! It belonged to Ponce de León.

Sting Ray: The Spanish explorer.

Liz Ard: You know your history.

Sting Ray: I also know that Ponce de León never traveled to Missouri. He died in Havana, Cuba, in 1521 after he was shot in the stomach with a poison arrow.

Liz Ard: That's where you're wrong. Ponce de León faked his death in Cuba and traveled northwest, searching for the Fountain of Youth.

Sting Ray: What makes you so sure?

Liz Ard: I had proof: his map, letters, and journals! He was convinced the Fountain of Youth was right here—in our little town!

Sting Ray: Funny. I don't remember ever hearing anything about this when you were town historian.

Liz Ard: I didn't tell anyone—except my stupid sister.

Sting Ray: Sally Mander.

Liz Ard: Yes. Biggest mistake of my life. I bragged to her about how close I was to discovering the Fountain of Youth. She told her pal Dee Eel. Next thing I knew, they'd moved to town and my map was gone. They stole it from me!

Sting Ray: The map didn't belong to you. It was city property. Why didn't you report it stolen?

Liz Ard: And admit to the whole town that I'd been keeping this information to myself? I couldn't come clean. Besides, Sally and Dee said they'd give me 30 percent of the take.

Sting Ray: A classic *quid pro quo.*

Liz Ard: Huh?

Sting Ray: Latin. It means "this for that." Your map for a share of their profits.

Liz Ard: Whatever.

Sting Ray: Keep talking.

Liz Ard: You know the rest. Sally ran for school board president.

Sting Ray: On a platform of building a new middle school.

Liz Ard: Right. According to the map, the Fountain of Youth was buried under the land now occupied by the middle school.

Sting Ray: Why build a school over it?

Liz Ard: You know how distracting kids are. Sally said we needed to camouflage our secret with a bunch of screaming brats.

Sting Ray: So Sally and Dee built the school using old junk they'd dug up around town.

Liz Ard: Yep. Too cheap to use new materials.

Sting Ray: And Dee built his water company next door to the school.

Liz Ard: He planned to bottle the water from the Fountain of Youth and sell it around the world.

Sting Ray: So they started drilling.

Liz Ard: Yes. And guess what they found? Water! Plain old springwater. Haw! Serves 'em right for stealing.

Sting Ray: You stole first, Liz Ard. You robbed this town of its place in history.

Liz Ard: But I never profited like Sally and Dee did. They didn't find the Fountain of Youth, but they made a bundle off their businesses.

Sting Ray: His water company and her swimming pool.

Liz Ard: Exactly. And they never gave me a thin dime of the profits. Their crimes paid. Mine never did. And besides—

Sting Ray: Besides nothing. Where were you the night Sally and Dee escaped?

Liz Ard: I was home all night. I took a bath around 9:30. Then I—

Sting Ray: Save your bad breath, Liz. I'm taking you downtown.

[SOUND OF HANDCUFFS LOCKING]

Sally Mander's Sister Arrested

Sting Ray says Liz Ard helped Sally and Dee escape.

Liz Ard, former town historian and Sally Mander's only sister, was arrested yesterday and charged with obstruction of justice, misappropriation of public documents and intent to defraud, said Lieut. Sting Ray, chief investigator with the Geyser Creek County Sheriff's Office.

Though he did not release a transcript of the interrogation, Ray gave the following account of his interview with Ard: "Liz Ard refused to cooperate with the investigation relating to the escape of her sister and Dee Eel from jail. Instead, she told a shaggy dog story about an alleged feud she had with her sister and Eel over a bogus map."

Ray bristled when reporters asked about the note Sally Mander left behind in her jail cell, stating that her sister, Liz Ard, "had nothing to do with this."

"I don't believe that for a New York minute," snapped Ray, who's leading the search for the missing felons. "I think the note was faked and that Liz Ard helped her sister and that slimy Eel escape. I'm just not sure what her motive was."

Liz ardently denied the charges, saying she was home taking a bath the night of the breakout. Ray reminded reporters: "It's not uncommon for criminals to invent alibis."

An *alibi* is a form of defense in which a defendant attempts to prove that he or she was elsewhere when the crime in question was committed. *Alibi* is Latin for "elsewhere."

How They Got Away with It

By Tad Poll, Investigative Reporter-in-Training

[Note: As a service to readers interested in journalism, we're printing Tad's stories as written by him and edited by me.
—Annette Trap, editor]

As we await the capture of Sally Mander and Delbert "Dee" Eel, many of us wonder how the villainous duo got away with their scam for so long.

"It's weird when you think that they fooled people in this town for 30 years," said Tad Poll. *[Tad, no quoting yourself, please. –A. T.]*

At this point in time we comprehend that Ms. Mander and Mr. Eel were not very honest. *[Write shorter, stronger sentences. –A. T.]*

Now we know that they were liars and cheats. *[Better! –A. T.]*

What we don't know is why Sally and Dee moved to town in the first place. What brought them here 31 years ago? And where are they now? *[No questions in news stories, Tad. If you don't know the answers, find out. –A. T.]*

Did y'all know?

Most criminal investigations involve identifying four elements: means, motive, opportunity and *modus operandi*. That's Latin for "method of operating."

Fowl Is Foul
Cafe Florence Opens to Complaints

New cafe has no bread for bread or donuts.

What should've been an opening-day celebration almost turned into a food fight yesterday at Cafe Florence, where the debut lunch special at the new eatery was chocolate chicken salad.

"I like to do the experiment with food," said the Italian-born Chef Angelo, who's learning English.

"From now on, experiment on yourself," said his wife and business partner, Angel Fisch, who became ill after trying the concoction.

Chef Angelo and Fisch were married on May 1. The newlyweds have reportedly been feuding ever since they decided to combine her cafe with his *caffè*.

Customers were disappointed by the new cafe's menu, and especially the absence of old favorites like Angel's famous glazed donuts.

"My sources tell me Chef Angelo goofed up the food order, and they didn't have any dough left for the donut ingredients," explained Sheriff Mack Rell. "Talk about a crime."

Now There's an Idea!
Idea box installed at courthouse

Summer intern Shelly is looking for a few good ideas.

The mayor's tourism task force hit upon a good idea at its first meeting last night.

"What we need is an idea box where people can submit their ideas for our town," said Mayor I. B. Newt.

The idea for the idea box came from the mayor's summer intern, Shelly, age 12.

"We were spinning our wheels, trying to think of ways to attract tourists to Geyser Creek," said Newt. "Then Shelly quietly said, 'Why don't we ask the people who live here for their ideas? If we make our town a nice place to live, it'll be a nice place to visit, too.'"

The idea box was installed at Geyser Creek City Hall.

"If you have an idea for how to make Geyser Creek a world-class town, just put the suggestion in the box," said Newt, who invited residents of Geyser Creek and the entire Jawlseedat Mountain region to use the new idea box at city hall.

The best ideas will be published daily in the *Gazette*.

June 27

NAME   **JOB**

Tad: Investigative reporter-in-training for the <u>Gazette</u>

Shelly: *Mayor Newt's summer intern*

Minnie O.:   *Researcher of GC's ancient history*

Gil: **Wally's administrative assistant**

Lily:
Paddy: We're still looking for jobs

Mr. N.:   School gardener. Anybody want to help me replant the garden?

TODAY'S ASSIGNMENT: How about studying a <u>foreign</u> WORD OF THE DAY? Maybe Latin?

Please, NO!!!!   It's summer!   Ugh!   NO WORD OF THE DAY!

Okay.
Design personal stationery for your summer job and write a letter to Florence.

Learn Latin

Garden

GEYSER CREEK'S MOST WANTED

Sally Mander

Delbert "Dee" Eel

? Whatever's eating Mr. N.'s garden

For the compost heap

Dear Florence, First, I want to tell you that Sally Mander and Dee Eel escaped from jail. A search is under way to find them. I also want to say that I hope you're having a nice summer over there in England, where your room in Bath is no doubt a million times nicer than our school bathrooms. (You don't even want to know about the basement bathrooms.) Finally, I should mention that I'm volunteering at the *Geyser Creek Gazette*. I'm learning how to write in the inverted pyramid style. There's this rule in journalism that says you put the biggest news at the top. Less important details are at the bottom of the story. See ya, Tad P.S. If you want, I'll sign you up for a summer subscription to the *Gazette*. When you're finished reading the paper, you can compost it for your garden. That's what Mr. N.'s doing.

SHELLY
Mayor I. B. Newt's Summer Intern
Geyser Creek City Hall
Geyser Creek, Missouri

June 27

Florence Waters
Our Far-flung Friend
4 Bubble Street
Bath, England

Hi, Florence!

I'll tell you one difference between Bath and Geyser Creek: tourism.

Every year Bath, England, attracts _millions_ of tourists. Know how many visitors we had last year in Geyser Creek? Ten. (And six of those were people who took wrong turns off the highway.)

So, I'm working with Mayor I. B. Newt on a tourism task force. He put me in charge of the new idea box at City Hall. It was my idea to ask people who live here to submit their ideas for making Geyser Creek and the entire Jawlseedat Mountain area not only a nice place to live but also a great place to visit.

So far we've received only one idea:

MY IDEA IS: The whole world's so stressed out these days. Let's make Geyser Creek a place that feels like summer all year long. People could come here and just be lazy. Wouldn't that be nice, y'all? Just thinking out loud here.   —Pearl O. Ster

The mayor rejected Pearl's idea on the basis that he didn't want to encourage "loafing around."

If you have any ideas about what we can do to attract tourists to Geyser Creek, let me know!

Yours truly, Shelly

Geyser Creek His, Hers, and Theirs-torical Society
"We dig your roots!"

206 Second Street   Geyser Creek, Missouri

Minnie O.
Summer Assistant

June 27

Ms. Florence Waters
Perennial Pen Pal
4 Bubble Street
Bath, England

Dear Florence,

I hope you're having a wonderful summer in Bath. I did some research and found out:

<u>Your Room in Bath</u> is in England. Bath is unique because it has the only natural hot springs in Britain.

34

<u>Our School Bathrooms</u> are located in a small town in Missouri named Geyser Creek, which sits in a valley shadowed by the Jawlseedat Mountain, about which little is known. Our basement bathrooms are unique because they are the dirtiest bathrooms in the school—maybe in the entire United States.

Love,

Minnie O.

P.S. As you can tell from my stationery, I've got a summer job at the Geyser Creek His, Hers, and Theirs-torical Society. Ms. Ologee asked me to research the ancient history of Geyser Creek and the whole Jawlseedat Mountain area. I can't wait!

Gil
Summer Intern

June 27

Ms. Florence Waters
Fountain Designer & Friend
4 Bubble Street
Bath, England

Hi, Florence!

I didn't know you have a house in Bath. *Bath* is such
a funny name for a town. Was the bathtub invented
there? Or maybe the hot tub?

Speaking of hot, Mr. N. is sorta steamed at us because
we vetoed the idea of doing any *real* schoolwork during
summer school. At first he suggested we study geology.
Then he suggested Latin. Huh? Shouldn't summer
school be just for FUN stuff?

Guess what else? I'm Wally's administrative assistant
for the summer. I'm trying to write his speech for the
SPA conference. It's supposed to be about his management philosophy: Work conquers all. (Is that true?)

I'm also supposed to ask you for an update on the
bathroom renovation project. Personally, I think trying
to fix up those gross restrooms in the basement is a lost
cause. Besides, there are so many other things we need
at school—like a gym and a library and an auditorium.

If *I* were renovating the school restrooms, I'd make
them rooms for all the REST of the things we need at
school.

REST (of the) ROOMS

BOYS   GIRLS

I'd also design a special executive restroom for Wally, where he could really *rest*.

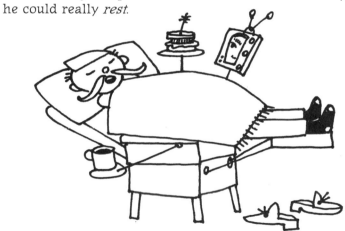

He's a nervous wreck about this SPA conference, in case you haven't noticed.

I'd better get back to work. Have fun in Bath!

Gil

Lily and **Paddy**
Chairmen of the BORED
Geyser Creek Middle School
Summer School
Geyser Creek, Missouri

June 27

Florence Waters
Fountain Designer and Our Favorite Pen Pal
4 Bubble Street
Bath, England

Hi, Florence!

I hope you're having a better summer than we are.

Everybody has a fun summer job except us. We offered to help Sheriff Mack Rell catch Sally Mander and Delbert "Dee" Eel. You heard those two escaped from jail, right?

Well, Sheriff Rell didn't want our help. So I guess it'll just be another boring summer in Geyser Creek.

Your Summer in Bath

FUN!

Relaxing

Filled with adventures

Our Summer in Geyser Creek

Backbreaking   Dull

Dum-di-dum-dum-dum

Boredly yours,
Lily   Paddy

38

Sam N.

Geyser Creek, Missouri

June 27

Ms. Florence Waters
4 Bubble Street
Bath, England

Dear Florence,

Can you tell it's summer school?

My students say they're "sick and tired" of schoolwork, especially WORD OF THE DAY, which they claim is the *world's most boring thing*. (I'm always the last to know.)

Also from the sick-and-tired department: Goldie. The poor thing has felt lousy ever since we returned from our honeymoon in Italy.

I packed a picnic lunch for us on Saturday and we hiked to the top of Jawlseedat Mountain. But Goldie couldn't eat a bite. She said she probably has the flu—or maybe picked up a bug in Italy.

Problem is, it's not flu season. And Goldie and I ate the exact same food on our honeymoon.

The bigger problem is that lately Goldie takes one look at me and then retreats to the bathroom.

I'm trying not to take all this personally, but I can't help wondering if Goldie thinks she made a mistake by marrying me.

Sorry to burden you with my problems. If you have any advice, I'd appreciate it.

Sign me,

Marriage Going Down the Toilet . . .

Sam N.

From My Bath Room

FLORENCE WATERS
4 BUBBLE STREET
BATH, ENGLAND

PRIORITY MAIL

July 1

Mr. Sam N.'s Classy Class
Summer School
Geyser Creek Middle School
Geyser Creek, Missouri USA

Dearest dearies,

Thanks for the lovely letters! I have them hanging in my Bath room. (And no, Gil, I don't have a house here in Bath, just a room. But who wouldn't love a Bath house?)

Like Geyser Creek, Bath has an amazing history. Beginning in the year AD 43, the Romans developed Bath as a city of recreation, relaxation, and rejuvenation. They built an elaborate series of baths around the hot springs to be used for cleansing and healing purposes—but mainly for fun!

Romans visited baths to swim and socialize.

apodyterium
(changing room)

tepidarium
(warm room)

Did you know they used olive oil instead of soap?

40

| caldarium | frigidarium | natatio |
| (hot room) | (cold room) | (swimming pool) |

Water was a constant temperature of 115° F. Bath temperature!

As the Roman Empire began to unravel in the fourth century, the baths were neglected. Eventually, through lack of maintenance and a failure in the drainage system, the baths flooded and were covered in thick black mud. They remained that way for more than a thousand years until the Victorians rediscovered the baths in 1880 and turned Bath into a popular tourist destination.

The baths are located below the modern street level.

Even now, Bath is a fabulous place to see Roman baths and to enjoy the therapeutic spa waters. Well, *usually* it is. The mood is very different in Bath this week. Looters are reportedly stealing priceless antiquities from the ancient ruins. What a pity.

In brighter news: Summer school sounds like fun! If you're still looking for something to study, consider my favorite subject: *gee*ology. It's the study of things that make you say, *"Gee, I didn't know that!"*

Whatever you do, please keep writing to me. I love reading your letters . . .

In my Bathroom, Florence

P.S. to Tad: I'd love a summer subscription to the *Gazette*. Thanks! You're smart to learn the rules of journalism. But don't be afraid to break the rules when circumstances demand.

P.P.S. to Shelly: An idea box! Brilliant. I'll try to think of ways to attract tourists to Geyser Creek while soaking in *my* idea box—the bathtub.

P.P.P.S. to Minnie O.: I never knew that lovely mountain overlooking Geyser Creek was called the Jawlseedat. I wonder how it got its name.

P.P.P.P.S. to Gil: Why *not* include a gymnasium, library, and all the *rest* in the basement restrooms? That would be perfectly traditional, which is what Wally wants. I'll handle his SPA speech.

P.P.P.P.P.S. to Lily and Paddy: How silly of Sheriff Mack Rell to decline your offer to help. Why don't you conduct your own investigations? I'm enclosing a parcel of my forensic equipment. Perhaps you could investigate the Case of the Dirty Basement Bathrooms. What's the story behind those lavatories?

P.P.P.P.P.P.S. to Sam: Poor Goldie. I'll send some Bath goodies to her in care of you. In the meantime, I suggest you draw her a bath.

July 5

Florence Waters
Fountain Designer and FANTASTIC Friend
4 Bubble Street
Bath, England

Dear Florence,

Thanks for the equipment. The carbon-dating device and DNA analysis kit look like so-o-o-o much fun!

You always cheer us up.

Boredly no moredly,

Lily   Paddy

P.S. Here's a coin we found when we were helping Mr. N. replant his garden behind school. Isn't it cool?

ⓘNTERPOL
International Criminal Police Organization
Lyon, France

Hugh Dunnit
Director of Investigations

9 July

Lily and Paddy
c/o Geyser Creek Middle School
Geyser Creek, Missouri USA

Lily and Paddy:

I am writing to you at the suggestion of Florence Waters.

For years Florence has volunteered for Interpol as a special
agent, helping in various international investigations. Often
she works as a mole, going undercover and infiltrating
unlawful—and sometimes lawful—organizations. Thanks to
Florence we've cracked many difficult cases.

I tried to convince Florence to help in a current investigation.
Unfortunately for us, she's on vacation. She gave me your
names as possible substitute investigators.

If you're interested in working for us on a case of international importance, please send me your CVs, along with a
letter of intent on your agency letterhead.

Thank you.

Hugh Dunnit

Hugh Dunnit

P.S. Florence forwarded the coin you sent her. It's almost
2,000 years old. Where on earth did you get it? As you'll see
from the attached news clip, it's likely stolen property.

BATH TIMES

June 22   The only (other) paper you need in Bath   **50 p**

Baths Closed

Online antiques market flooded with rare archaeological finds

Rare antiquities offered online.

Authorities in Bath are baffled by the appearance of ancient flints, coins, pottery and other valuable antiquities on Internet auction sites.

"From the pictures I've seen, many of the antiquities look suspiciously similar to what we have here in Bath," said Anita Shawer, Bath's chief of police.

Concerned that looters may be pilfering Bath's ruins, authorities closed the famous baths of Bath today.

"The baths will remain closed until we can take inventory of the site and determine if there has been looting in the baths," said Shawer.

The antiquities began appearing online a year ago. The source of these rarities is unknown because online sales are confidential. Internet auction houses protect the identity of both the seller and the buyer involved in each transaction.

Online auction brokers say that barring evidence that the antiquities are stolen, they will continue to allow the items in question to be sold over the Internet.

"Looting of historic baths is not uncommon, given the demand for stolen antiquities and the high prices they command in the underground economy," said Rob R. Dukky, an authority on ancient baths.

Early Risers Enjoy Solstice Sunrise at Stonehenge

Sunrise at Stonehenge attracts onlookers.

Thousands gathered yesterday to watch the summer solstice sunrise at Stonehenge, a formation of huge rocks constructed 5,000 years ago.

"It's just about the loveliest thing I've ever seen," said international designer Lorence Waters, who traveled from nearby Bath to witness the annual spectacle.

Although there is some debate about the origins of Stonehenge, most archaeologists agree the monument was built for worship ceremonies. The circular arrangement of the stones also suggests possible astronomical uses, such as tracking the movements of stars and planets.

Anita Shawer closes the baths of Bath.

July 12

Mr. Hugh Dunnit
Director of Investigations
Interpol
Lyon, France

Dear Mr. Dunnit,

We had **NO** idea the coin we sent Florence was stolen. We found it behind the local middle school here in Geyser Creek.

We also had no idea Florence was an investigator and a mole. But we're not at all surprised. Florence can do anything!

Anyway, our agency is <u>VERY</u> interested in working for you. Please tell us how we can help. Our firm is not very old, but we hope you agree that youth has its advantages.

At your service,

Agent Lily   Agent Paddy

P.S. We'd be happy to provide our CVs if you'll kindly tell us what they are.

ⓘNTERPOL
International Criminal Police Organization
Lyon, France

Hugh Dunnit
Director of Investigations

15 July

Lily Pad's Private Investigations, Etc.
c/o Geyser Creek Middle School
Geyser Creek, Missouri USA

Agents Lily and Paddy:

Thank you for your prompt reply.

Please begin your investigation by searching for other antiquities (ancient coins, pottery, tools, etc.) near the site where you discovered the coin. International looters could be using an unlikely location, such as a small town in the United States, to stash these stolen goods.

Also, please alert local authorities to the possible presence of an international crime ring in your area.

Very clever to base your operations in the most uneventful of spots: an American middle school.

Hugh Dunnit

Hugh Dunnit

P.S. *CV* is short for *curriculum vitae*, which is Latin for the "course of one's life or career." Interpol procedure demands that you provide some basic background information, such as your place and date of birth, education, and professional experience.

P.P.S. By the way, *P.S.* is an abbreviation for the Latin *post scriptum,* which means "written after."

47

July 18

Sheriff Mack Rell
Geyser Creek Sheriff's Office
Geyser Creek, Missouri

ADVISORY: Possible criminal activity in Geyser Creek

We have reason to believe members of an international crime ring are hiding stolen antiquities (that means valuable old stuff, like coins and broken pots and statues and things) in Geyser Creek until they can sell them online for lots of money.

We know it sounds crazy, but we thought you should know.

Agent Lily   Agent Paddy

P.S. If you change your mind about letting us help with the search for Sally Mander and Dee Eel, just holler. We've formed a PI agency!

July 19

Lily and Paddy
Geyser Creek Middle School
Summer School
Geyser Creek, Missouri

Dear Lily and Paddy,

Girls, girls, girls. You've been reading too
many kid detective stories. Pip-squeaks can't
solve tough cases like this. They require
~~perfessional~~ ~~purrfeshional~~ really good
investigators like Sting and me.

So just leave the serious crime-solving to us.
We'll give you the straight poop on the case
after we get Sally and Dee back in the slammer,
where they belong.

Mack Rell

Mack Rell

P.S. If you want to help, how 'bout tracking
down my car keys for me? I can't find the dang
things anywhere.

49

HAND DELIVERED

July 20

Sheriff Mack Rell
Geyser Creek Sheriff's Office
Geyser Creek, Missouri

Herewith our report on the Case of Your Missing Car Keys:

THE FACTS: After determining that you must've had your car keys yesterday (because you drove to work), we searched your office without success. We then asked you to search your pockets, also without success. Finally, we asked permission to search your car—and we found your keys in the ignition.

This concludes our report.

Agent Lily   Agent Paddy

P.S. We really wish you'd let us help with the search for Sally and Dee. We also think you should consider using a computer that has a spell-checking feature.

MACK RELL
Sheriff

July 20

Lily and Paddy
Geyser Creek Middle School
Summer School
Geyser Creek, Missouri

Lily and Paddy,

Dang-it-all, girls, I can't let you help with
the investigation. The rules don't permit it.

But thanks for finding my car keys for me! I
forgot I took a nap out there yesterday.

Mack Rell

Mack Rell

P.S. I'm too old to learn how to operate a
fancy computer. This typewriter's good enough
for me.

NAME   **JOB**

Tad: Investigative reporter-in-training for the Gazette

Shelly: *Mayor Newt's summer intern*

Minnie O.: *Researching GC's ancient history*

Anybody know how the Pawlseedat Mountain got its name?

Gil: Wally's administrative assistant

Lily:

Paddy: *International crime solving*

Mr. N.: Re-replanting the garden

TODAY'S ASSIGNMENT: Spend as much class time at your job as necessary. We'll keep in touch via letters.

Will someone please deliver this to Goldie? She still feels queasy at the sight of me.

Flo W.
Mrs Buch Plan
Bath, England

To: Goldie Fisch N
c/o Mrs Sam N
Grimmel School
Geyser Creek
Middle School
Geyser Creek, Mo USA

Please bring in newspapers for compost.

CREEK'S
WANTED

For the compost heap

Sally Mander

Delbert "Dee" Eel

? Whatever's STILL eating Mr. N.'s garden

GOLDIE FISCH-N.

July 21

Florence Waters
Friend, Adviser, and Confidante
4 Bubble Street
Bath, England

Dear Florence,

You're so sweet to send me the wonderful gifts from Bath. The scones are scrumptious! And I can't wait to try the bath salts from Bath! Thank you.

I guess Sam told you that I'm not feeling so great. Florence, I don't know what to do. I thought being married to Sam would make me happy. So far all it's made me is sick.

I shouldn't complain. At least Sam and I are still speaking. Angel moved out of the apartment you built for her and Chef Angelo in the hall tree. She's living in Springfield now. I'm afraid their marriage is really on the rocks. Working together at Cafe Florence has been tough on their relationship. My sister was used to running things *her* way at Geyser Creek Cafe. No one *ever* complained about her cooking. But when Angelo cooks? Well, it's a different story. You don't even want to know about how he smelled up the whole town last week when he tried to hard-boil eggs. It *still* stinks around here.

But do you know what really stinks? Gaining weight. Since the wedding, I've packed on *nine* pounds. (Ugh!) It must have been all that pasta and gelato I ate in Italy. I'm hiring a personal trainer tomorrow!

Gosh, I'm sorry to be such a complainer. I'm never this moody. I wonder what's wrong with me.

Love,

Goldie

P.S. Gil delivered your package to me. Poor kid. He said Wally's been yelling at him about not having his SPA speech written. I'm going to call that man right now!

From the Principal's Desk
Labor omnia vincit.
(Work conquers all.)

Mr. Walter Russ
Principal

July 21

Florence Waters
President, Flowing Waters Fountains, Etc.
4 Bubble Street
Bath, England

Ms. Waters,

I just received a distressing phone call from your friend Goldie Fisch-N., who began berating me for unknown reasons. Then she burst into tears and hung up on me.

In any case, Gil has informed me that you've agreed to write my speech for the SPA conference. (Thank you.) I've been struggling with the title of my speech. Here are my ideas so far:

- The Ten Habits of Highly Feared Principals
- The Principal Never Smiles
- Meetings Make the Manager!
- Don't Ask, Just Yell
- Task-Force Your Way to the Top
- All Work and No Play: Who Said Being Principal Was Going to Be *Fun*?

Please use one of these titles for my speech and send me a rough draft for review. Something sketchy is fine. It's important that the speech reflects my management philosophy: *Labor omnia vincit* ("Work conquers all").

As you know, I'm also relying on you to renovate the basement bathrooms before the principals and administrators arrive for the SPA conference. They're really in terrible shape. The bathrooms, I mean. Not the principals and administrators.

Sorry so disjointed. I'm under a lot of pressure lately.

Gotta run.

Walter Russ

FLORENCE WATERS
4 BUBBLE STREET
BATH, ENGLAND

~~PRIORITY MAIL~~

July 25

Wally Russ
The Principal Who's Gotta Run (to the bathroom)
Geyser Creek Middle School
Geyser Creek, Missouri USA

Dear Wallykins,

So sorry to hear you've got the runs. Do you think your loose bowels might be stress related? It's often the case, you know.

Well, don't worry about your SPA speech. It's coming along quite nicely. I've decided the speech will reflect your *new* management philosophy. More on that anon.

Given your current (*ahem*) condition, I suggest you deliver the speech from the basement restrooms. Gil has some wonderful ideas for the renovation. Here's something sketchy.

The rest will be a surprise!

Hope you feel better soon, Wally.

Florence

From the Principal's Desk

Labor omnia vincit.

(Work conquers all.)

Mr. Walter Russ
Principal

OVERNIGHT MAIL

July 27

Florence Waters
President, Flowing Waters Fountains, Etc.
4 Bubble Street
Bath, England

Ms. Waters,

I do *not* have loose bowels.

Nor do I have any intention of giving my speech to the Society of Principals and Administrators (SPA) in the school *bathrooms*.

Nor do I need or want a new management philosophy.

Walter Russ

P.S. I don't like surprises, either. I gotta go.

From My Bath Room To Yours!

FLORENCE WATERS
4 BUBBLE STREET
BATH, ENGLAND

July 28

EXPRESS MAIL

Wally Russ
My Absoloooootely Favorite Principal
Geyser Creek Middle School
Geyser Creek, Missouri

Poor Wally.

You've gotta go? I take it you mean you don't have the runs, but the *opposite* problem.

Well, I can't say that I'm surprised.

You looked a little puffy and pasty in May at our nonwedding. I didn't say anything about it at the time because I didn't think it was any of my business. But I couldn't help wondering.

And then your unpleasant letters this summer had such an uptight tone. Your increasingly shaky handwriting was a give-away. Again, I hardly thought it my place to ask about the . . . problem. But since you've brought it up.

Wally, constipation can *also* be caused by stress and an unhealthy diet. Are you drinking enough water? Are you eating fresh fruits and veggies? What about fiber? Exercise? Are you getting outside and playing a little every day?

The good news, Wally, is that this problem is solvable—and is all the more reason to hold the SPA conference in the school bathrooms.

Now don't worry about a thing. Just skip to the loo, my darling. And don't come out until you're finished.

Yours in Bath,

Florence

P.S. A dear friend of mine has an organic prune farm. I'm ordering a truckload of the finest prunes sent to you ASAP.

From the Principal's Desk

Labor omnia vincit.

(Work conquers all.)

Mr. Walter Russ
Principal

OVERNIGHT MAIL

July 29

Florence Waters
President, Flowing Waters Fountains, Etc.
4 Bubble Street
Bath, England

Ms. Waters!

Please do not concern yourself with my . . . plumbing!

The only bowels you need to worry about are the bowels of the school, where some bathrooms are in dire need of renovation.

About my speech: Can I *please* see a rough outline of what you're working on? I'm sorry to be so insistent, but I'm trying to put my best foot forward at this conference.

Walter Russ

P.S. I'm glad some people have time to go on vacation while the rest of us have to *work* for a living.

P.P.S. I don't like prunes.

From My Bath Room To Yours!

FLORENCE WATERS
4 BUBBLE STREET
BATH, ENGLAND

July 30

EXPRESS MAIL

Wally Russ
The Principal Who Needs a Re-laxative
Geyser Creek Middle School
Geyser Creek, Missouri

Wally,

If you must know what I'm working on at the moment, I'll tell you: my toenails. Here's a rough outline:

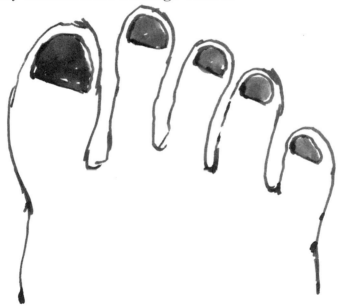

If you want to put your best foot forward for the SPA conference, I suggest you get a spa pedicure, too, like me. And be sure to ask for a foot massage. Reflexology can be wonderful for curing (and preventing) constipation.

Wally, do you know what your problem is? You WORK too hard. And that never works, does it?

Guess what I do when I have an important job: I go on vacation. Did you know that *vacation* comes from the Latin word *vacare,* which means "to be empty"? Sometimes you have to empty your mind of old thoughts and habits to free it up for *new* ideas. And sometimes doing nothing (often called meditating, from the Latin word *meditari*) connects you to something very powerful that can fill you back up.

Will you try something for me? Just sit still and be quiet for a minute. WALLY! You're fidgeting. I can feel it. Stop it.

Sit still and be silent. Now focus on your breathing. Breathe in and say *Ohhhhhhhhh*. Then breathe out and say *Kaaaaayyyyyyyyy*.

Start by doing this for five minutes a day. Work up to 20 minutes. Every day. Okay? You must learn to relax and let go. It will cure so many of your problems.

Wally, you know what else you need? A nice soak in the tub. Please take two hot baths and write to me in the morning.

Doctor Flo W.

Here's a footnote to this foot note: I'm enclosing some bath toys from Bath for you.

P.S. Did you know the word *laxative* comes from the Latin verb *laxare,* which means "to loosen"? In other words, Wally, *loosen up*!

From the Principal's Desk

Labor omnia vincit.

(Work conquers all.)

Mr. Walter Russ
Principal

OVERNIGHT MAIL

August 1

Florence Waters
President, Flowing Waters Fountains, Etc.
4 Bubble Street
Bath, England

Ms. Waters:

I do not have time to sit still, relax, loosen up, and do *nothing.*
Nor do I have time for a spa pedicure, foot massage, and/or
a nice hot *bath*—with or without Bath toys.

Because you refuse to cooperate with my simple requests, I'll
find someone else to renovate the basement bathrooms and
write my speech. (I'd write the stupid thing myself, but I'm
completely blocked.)

Enjoy your bath.

Walter Russ

P.S. In case the above is not sufficiently clear—YOU'RE
CANNED!

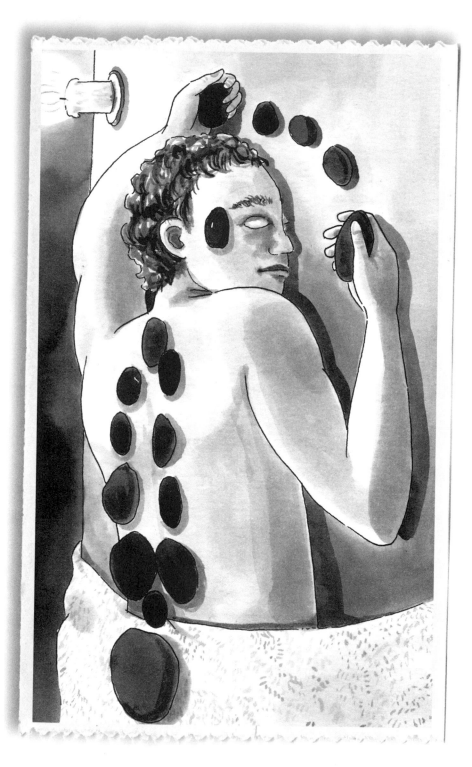

Hot stone therapy has been used for thousands of years to harmonize and relax the body.

August 2

Wally,

"Wally" is such a crass term. When to say I'm on the throne, I prefer the throne.

But Wally, listen to me. If you have a complete blockage, you must see a doctor immediately. A blocked bowel can be very dangerous.

Wally Knox

Who can make such a fuss?

Enjoy Creek Middle School
Wiggle Creek
Enjoy, Minnesota
USA

87.80

AIR MAIL

BATH
£0.47

BATH
2
AUG
A.M.
ENGLAND

GEYSER CREEK MIDDLE SCHOOL
From the Principal's Desk
Labor omnia vincit.
(Work conquers all.)

Mr. Walter Russ
Principal

OVERNIGHT MAIL

August 3

Florence Waters
President, Flowing Waters Fountains, Etc.
4 Bubble Street
Bath, England

Ms. Waters:

Now hold it just one minute. By *canned* I meant you are
relieved of your duties. You are *eliminated* from this project.

And that's the bottom line.

Walter Russ

P.S. My blockage is none of your business.

From My Bath Room To Yours!

FLORENCE WATERS
4 BUBBLE STREET
BATH, ENGLAND

August 4

Wally Russ
Mister Potty-Mouth Principal
Geyser Creek Middle School
Geyser Creek, Missouri

EXPRESS MAIL

Oh, Wally.

Just because you're constipated doesn't mean you can tell *me* to hold it. I *never* hold it. That's why I'm always *relieved* of my "duties," as you call them.

So let's concentrate on relieving you of *your* "duties," shall we?

Wally, you're a grown man, and if you don't want to see a doctor about your blocked bowel, that's your business. There's no need to get nasty about it. (Don't worry. I won't take it personally. I know it's part of your . . . condition.)

And I suppose it's healthy that you're comfortable discussing bodily functions, like *elimination*. But it can get a bit tiresome.

Now, regarding the bathrooms: What's your feeling about towel racks? Do you like these?

Never mind. Don't worry about the details. I'll take care of everything.

See you soon!

Florence

P.S. You and your bottom line, Wally. Really!

MEMO

DATE: AUGUST 5

TO: GIL

FR: PRINCIPAL WALTER RUSS

RE: THE BATHROOMS

Whether she realizes it or not, I have fired Florence Waters. That means you are now in charge of writing my speech *and* finding someone to renovate the basement bathrooms in a traditional style before the SPA conference on August 31.

I'll also need a haircut before the conference. Please book an appointment for me with Fisher Cutbait.

I'll be back later this afternoon. I have an appointment in Springfield regarding a . . . personal matter.

You may help yourself to the prunes on my desk.

Gladys Ownleepoup, MD

Springfield, Missouri

2 Porsa Lane

Patient name: Walter Russ
Date of visit: August 5
Diagnosis: Severe constipation
Possible cause(s): Stress

Rx:

Try to take care of this matter yourself, Walter. If you can't, we'll have to surgically remove the blockage.

Gladys Ownleepoup, MD

☆THE GEYSER CREEK GAZETTE☆

Our motto: "We have a nose for news!"

| Saturday, August 6 | Early Edition | 50 cents |

Mander and Eel Investigation Ongoing

By Tad Poll, Investigative Reporter-in-Training
(with editorial assistance from Annette Trap)

Sally Mander and Delbert "Dee" Eel are still being looked for by authorities. *[Tad, use the active voice instead of the passive. –A. T.]*

Authorities are still searching for escaped convicts Sally Mander and Delbert "Dee" Eel. *[Much better! –A. T.]*

Investigator Lieut. Sting Ray said that though clues are scarce, the trail is still warm.

"This is not a cold case," said Ray, who refused to discuss the matter in detail. "It's not unusual for escaped cons to follow coverage of their cases in the local media. We don't want to provide Mander and Eel with regular updates on the investigation."

Lieut. Sting Ray continues to search for Mander and Eel.

Principal Goes to the Bathroom

By Tad Poll, Investigative Reporter-in-Training
(with editorial assistance from Annette Trap)

Due to health concerns, Principal Walter Russ is planning the upcoming conference of the Society of Principals and Administrators (SPA) from the faculty restroom at Geyser Creek Middle School.

Though Russ was unavailable for comment, his administrative assistant said that yesterday Russ visited a Springfield doctor, who instructed him to "take care of this matter." Otherwise, surgery will be necessary.

The problem is that, even though he's in the bathroom, Principal Walter Russ can't go to the bathroom. *[Tad, no euphemisms in journalism. –A. T.]* The condition is believed to be stress related. *[Vague, but okay. –A. T.]*

Russ has been under a lot of pressure lately. He wants to have the school's basement bathrooms renovated in time for the SPA conference on August 31. According to sources, Russ is also worried about the speech he's preparing for 300 visiting principals and administrators, as well as the banquet slated to follow the speech.

Chef Angelo offers to help Principal Russ with the banquet.

Chef Angelo has offered to help.

"I must to show my wife, the Angel, that I am not the big head with knuckles she says that I am," Chef Angelo told Russ through the locked restroom door.

(Continued on page 2, column 2)

Angel Fisch Files for Divorce

Fisch throws in the towel on marriage to Chef Angelo—and on Cafe Florence.

Citing irreconcilable differences and her refusal to be married to a "complete and total knucklehead," Angel Fisch filed for divorce from Chef Angelo yesterday.

In divorce papers filed at Geyser Creek County Courthouse, Fisch and her attorney, Barry Cuda, outlined her grievances, including "the fact that my husband goofed up our summer food order, stank up the whole town with the smell of rotten eggs and has made me so sick I've been puking my guts up for a month."

Angel Fisch and Chef Angelo were married on May 1 in a double ceremony with her sister, Goldie Fisch, and Sam N. That marriage is also reportedly in the toilet and headed toward divorce.

IDEA BOX

Here are today's best ideas submitted to the idea box.

As compiled by Shelly, Mayor I. B. Newt's summer intern

MY IDEA IS: We make Geyser Creek the city where people who have the problems with the marriage they can come and fall in the big happy love again. Make Geyser Creek the city for the second moon of honey. That is my wish for Geyser Creek and what I want for me and my wife, the beautiful Angel. —Chef Angelo

MY IDEA IS: We give folks what they really want: a place where they can go and get a quickie divorce. Give special discounts to women like me who are married to knuckleheads and *penne* pinchers! —Angel Fisch

School Garden Gobbled Again

Teacher blames moles

Students find tunnels, flints in garden.

Corn. Lettuce. Baby carrots.

These are just a few of the vegetables that will have to be replanted for a third time after varmints gobbled the goodies in the Geyser Creek Middle School's summer garden.

Summer school teacher Sam N. blamed moles for the damage.

"You can tell it's moles by the tunneling," said Sam N.

In addition to finding mole damage, one student uncovered several flints in the garden dirt yesterday.

"They look real old," said Shelly, who turned the prehistoric artifacts over to Minnie O., summer intern with the Geyser Creek His, Hers, and Theirs-torical Society.

Did y'all know?

Humans have been making tools for at least 2.5 million years. The earliest tools were fashioned from pebbles and used to chop, cut and scrape.

PRINCIPAL *(Continued from page 1, column 2)*

Due to a mistake in a food order, Chef Angelo has only eggs, chicken, chocolate and his collection of spices to cook with this summer.

"Maybe I make the scrambly curry eggs with the chocolate chips," he suggested.

With a faint "No," Russ vetoed that idea from the faculty restroom.

[Nicely done, Tad. It's not easy to write a tasteful story about a principal with severe constipation. –A. T.]

Sorry for the bad smelly yesterday.
I overboil the eggs hard again.

I love you, sweet Angel.
— Chef Angelo

For Sale
Wedding Ring
barely used ◆ microscopic diamond
Contact Angel Fisch

Fisher Cutbait
Barber
Going on vacation
I'll be back September 1.

Lily Pad's
Private Investigations, Etc.
c/o Geyser Creek Middle School
Geyser Creek, Missouri

August 8

Minnie O.
Summer Assistant
Geyser Creek His, Hers, and Theirs-torical Society
206 Second Street
Geyser Creek, Missouri

Hey, Minnie O.!

Can we come by sometime to look at those flints Shelly
found in the garden? Florence sent us some equipment that
can help us determine how old they are.

Hope you're having fun researching the ancient history of
Geyser Creek. Did anyone respond to your newspaper ad?

Lily   Paddy

P.S. Do you want to join our PI firm?

71

Geyser Creek His, Hers, and Theirs-torical Society
"We dig your roots!"

206 Second Street   Geyser Creek, Missouri

Minnie O.
Summer Assistant

August 9

Lily and Paddy
Lily Pad's Private Investigations, Etc.
c/o Geyser Creek Middle School
Geyser Creek, Missouri

Dear Lily and Paddy,

Thanks for your letter. Come over anytime to look at the flints. I'd love to know how old they are. Maybe it'll help with my research project, which is going terribly.

The only response I've gotten to my newspaper ad was a phone call from Pearl, who wanted me to come over to her beauty shop and visit. Pearl's so nice, but she doesn't understand that I don't have time to visit. I'm trying to work!

I'm getting really stressed out by this job.

Minnie O.

P.S. I'd love to join your private investigation company, if I have time.

Lily Pad's
Private Investigations, Etc.
c/o Geyser Creek Middle School
Geyser Creek, Missouri

Founders and Agents: Lily and Paddy
His, Hers, and Theirs-torical Research: Minnie O.

August 10

Mr. Hugh Dunnit
Director of Investigations
Interpol
Lyon, France

Mr. Dunnit,

This is an official report from Geyser Creek:

At approximately 1400 hours last Friday, several flints (aka prehistoric artifacts) were discovered in a vegetable garden behind Geyser Creek Middle School. Based on our analysis (see attached report), these flints were made by hand in the year 10,000 BC. One flint appears to be a spear point similar to those used by the Paleoindians.

This concludes our report.

Bye for now!

Agent Lily   Agent Paddy

P.S. As you can see from our letterhead, we've expanded our firm. We're still working on our CVs.

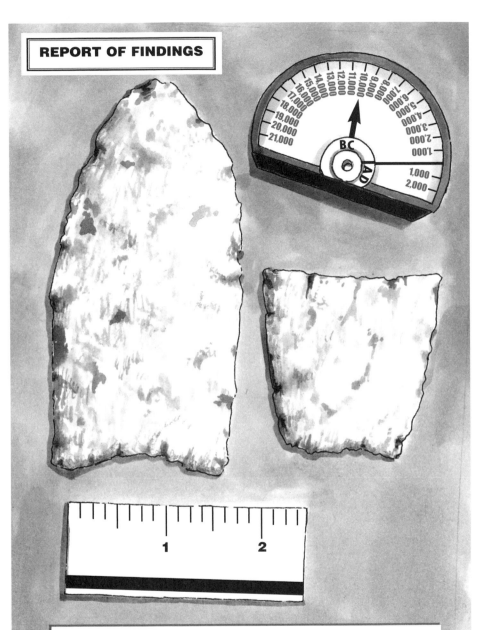

REPORT OF FINDINGS

Background on Paleoindians: Scientific evidence suggests the earliest Americans were descendants of Asian hunters who followed herds of migrating caribou, mammoths, and other Ice Age mammals across the Bering Land Bridge from Asia to Alaska. Spear points embedded in the remains of mastodons indicate Paleoindians were in the United States twelve thousand years ago.

(i)NTERPOL

International Criminal Police Organization

Lyon, France

Hugh Dunnit
Director of Investigations

12 August

Lily Pad's Private Investigations, Etc.
c/o Geyser Creek Middle School
Geyser Creek, Missouri USA

Agents Lily and Paddy:

Excellent work. Your research shows that the artifacts stashed in Geyser Creek were excavated from a site even older than Bath. It's obvious that Geyser Creek has become a storage site for looters who are stealing rare antiquities and selling them via Internet auction sites.

Two questions remain: Who are the looters? Where are they getting these prehistoric artifacts?

I have one bit of new information. See below.

Who's Selling Antiquities Online?
Dasyatislata, that's who

BATH, England—Authorities have a new clue about the identity of the antiquities dealer selling historical artifacts online: namely, his or her online screen name, *Dasyatislata*.

"Clearly it's a secret code," said Hugh Dunnit, director of investigations for Interpol, the international police organization. "Our cryptologists are working around the clock to decode it."

A judge in London is reviewing requests by Interpol to subpoena records from Internet auction houses, which thus far have maintained their right to protect the identity of their buyers and sellers.

Please continue digging for more information while focusing on our key questions. And do let your local law enforcement officials know of your recent findings.

Hugh Dunnit

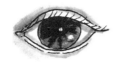

Lily Pad's
Private Investigations, Etc.
c/o **Geyser Creek Middle School**
Geyser Creek, Missouri

Founders and Agents: Lily and Paddy
His, Hers, and Theirs-torical Research: Minnie O.

August 15

Lieut. Sting Ray
Investigator
Geyser Creek Sheriff's Office
Geyser Creek, Missouri

Lieutenant Ray,

Believe it or not, international looters might be using Geyser Creek to hide stolen antiquities. We don't know who the looters are, but our source tells us that they're using the computer screen name *Dasyatislata*.

Just thought you should know. We tried to tell Sheriff Mack Rell this, but he seems more interested in donuts.

Agent Lily   Agent Paddy

P.S. We're working on a pretty big case for Interpol, but if you need help finding Sally and Dee, we'll make time for that!

Geyser
Creek
Sheriff's
Office

Geyser Creek

MISSOURI

August 16

Lily and Paddy
Lily Pad's Private Investigations, Etc.
c/o Geyser Creek Middle School
Geyser Creek, Missouri

Dear Lily and Paddy,

You're right about Sheriff Mack Rell. His laid-back management style might be comical if the safety of this town and its citizens weren't at stake.

For decades the sheriff has taken a hands-off approach to Sally Mander and Dee Eel that I find both troubling and curious. If you didn't know better, you might think Sheriff Mack was on their side.

Is it any wonder that international looters have set up shop in a town with a joke of a sheriff? I hope you can do something about this.

I also hope you'll join the search for Sally Mander and Dee Eel—with or without Sheriff Mack Rell's permission.

Sting Ray
Sting Ray

Lily Pad's
Private Investigations, Etc.
c/o Geyser Creek Middle School
Geyser Creek, Missouri

Founders and Agents: Lily and Paddy
His, Hers, and Theirs-torical Research: Minnie O.

August 17

Tad Poll
Investigative Reporter-in-Training
The Geyser Creek Gazette
Geyser Creek, Missouri

Tad,

Take a look at this letter we just got from Sting Ray.

Maybe this is crazy, but do you think Sheriff Mack Rell might be protecting Sally Mander and Dee Eel? Mack could've been their mole all these years.

In case you didn't know, a <u>mole</u> is someone who infiltrates an organization to gather inside information.

What do you think?

Lily   Paddy

P.S. Want to join our PI firm? Ask Shelly, too, if you see her.

August 18

Lily and Paddy
Lily Pad's Private Investigations, Etc.
c/o Geyser Creek Middle School
Geyser Creek, Missouri

Lily and Paddy,

Wow. And very weird.

I'll try to interview Mack tonight.

Tad Poll

P.S. Of course I want to join your PI firm. Shelly's sitting right next to me, working on her next article. She says she's in, too.

INTERVIEW WITH
SHERIFF MACK RELL

TRANSCRIPT

Tad Poll: Sheriff Rell, I'd like to interview you for the *Gazette*.

Mack Rell: Okay. What do you wanna know, kiddo?

Tad Poll: Cut the good-old-boy routine, Sheriff. I have reason to believe you're a mole.

Mack Rell: A *mole*? Well, I'll be dadgummed. I know I ain't no oil painting. But calling me a mole is a little salty, kid.

Tad Poll: I mean an infiltrator.

Mack Rell: Infil-*who*?

Tad Poll: Someone who burrows inside an organization for legal or illegal purposes. I think you were Sally and Dee's mole here in Geyser Creek. You knew what they were up to all those years. But you protected them, possibly for money.

Mack Rell: You're losing me, kid. A mole's a varmint, ain't it? Like a chipmunk. If I was a mole, how would I even know how to use a telephone? You ever seen a mole making a phone call?

Tad Poll: Sheriff, I don't mean to be disrespectful, but are you really as dim as you seem?

Mack Rell: Is this a trick question?

Tad Poll: Never mind.

Progress Report on Summer Jobs

Name	Working on
Tad:	Investigative reporter-in-training for the Gazette
Shelly:	*Mayor Newt's summer intern*
Minnie O.:	*Trying to dig up info on GC's ancient history*
Gil:	**Writing Wally's speech**
	Delivering Wally's mail to faculty restroom
	Planning SPA banquet with Chef Angelo
	Trying to find someone to cut Wally's hair
	Trying to find contractor for bathroom renovation
	Worrying about all of the above
Lily/Paddy:	Sleuthing
Mr. N.:	**Trying to save my garden and my marriage**

TODAY'S ASSIGNMENT: Please research one of the following:

- **how to trap moles**
- **tips on how to be a better husband**
- **divorce rate among newlyweds**

SHELLY
Mayor I. B. Newt's Summer Intern
Geyser Creek City Hall
Geyser Creek, Missouri

August 19

Mr. N.,

Here are some ideas for eliminating moles and saving your marriage.

<u>Gardeners use the following as mole repellents:</u>

<u>You could give Goldie:</u>

rose branches

roses

mothballs

gum balls

lye

NO lies

dead fish

lobster dinner

human hair

You could brush her hair?

Shelly

82

Geyser Creek His, Hers, and Theirs-torical Society
"We dig your roots!"

206 Second Street   Geyser Creek, Missouri

Minnie O.
Summer Assistant

August 19

Dear Mr. N.,

The U.S. Census does not track the national divorce rate among newlyweds. But I conducted a local poll and found only one other newlywed couple: Chef Angelo and Angel Fisch. They're having even more problems than you and Goldie.

If you all get divorced, Geyser Creek will have a 100% divorce rate for newlyweds.

Personally, Mr. N., I think that would be tragic.

Minnie O.

Lily Pad's
Private Investigations, Etc.
c/o Geyser Creek Middle School
Geyser Creek, Missouri

Founders and Agents: Lily and Paddy
His, Hers, and Theirs-torical Research: Minnie O.
Investigative Research: Tad Poll
Director of Ideas: Shelly

August 19

Mr. N.

Our research indicates that moles are carnivores. Thus, they are not responsible for the damage to your vegetable garden.

With your permission, we will keep digging to find what's eating your vegetables.

Don't worry, Mr. N. We'll help you save your garden. You're on your own with Goldie.

Lily   Paddy

84

TAD POLL
Investigative Reporter-in-Training
THE GEYSER CREEK GAZETTE
"We have a nose for news!"

August 19

Mr. N.,

I've obviously never been married. (I don't even have a girlfriend.) And you know I'm not a tattletale, right? But I thought I should you tell you this:

I saw your wife, Goldie, walking very quickly down Main Street yesterday with a very athletic-looking man. I stopped to say hi, but Goldie said she couldn't chat. She practically *ran* away from me with the man.

I've known Goldie since I was in fourth grade, and I've never known her not to stop and say hello.

But here's the strangest thing: Goldie had a glow about her that I've never seen before—except on the day she married you.

I'm sorry to be the bearer of bad news. You asked for tips on how to be a better husband. I'm afraid it might be too late.

Tad Poll

FROM THE DESK OF GIL
Administrative Assistant to Principal Walter Russ
Geyser Creek Middle School   Geyser Creek, Missouri

Gil
Summer Intern

August 19

Florence Waters
Fountain Designer and Friend
4 Bubble Street
Bath, England

Dear Florence,

I'm supposed to be working on a class assignment,
but I need someone to talk to, so I'm writing to you.

I always wanted a job because I thought it would
make me feel like a grown-up. But working as Wally's
administrative assistant this summer just makes me
feel like the dumbest kid in town.

I can't do anything right. I can't write a speech, like
Wally wants me to. I was supposed to make an
appointment for him to get a haircut, but Fisher
Cutbait is on vacation. And worst of all, I haven't
found anyone who can renovate the basement
bathrooms in time for the SPA conference. I can't
even find someone who will *clean* them. (That's how
bad they are.)

Today I went down to the basement and tried to tackle
the job myself. The frustrating part is that I keep
washing the bathroom walls, but I can't get them
clean. There's graffiti scrawled all over them that just
won't come off. And guess who volunteered to help
me? Nobody.

86

I can't say that I blame the other kids in my class. They all have cool summer jobs. Plus, they've formed some sort of private investigation firm. Guess who asked me to join? Nobody. Probably because they know I'm such a crummy worker.

I hope you're having a better summer than I am. I wish you were still coming for the SPA conference. But now that Wally's fired you, I guess you're not.

Don't feel bad. He'll fire me, too—as soon as he comes out of the faculty bathroom and finds out I've failed at every job he's given me.

Gil

P.S. I told Mr. N. that I was worried about getting fired. He said, "Join the club." I hate to spread gossip, but the word on the street is that Goldie's going to dump Mr. N. for a new guy. Mr. N.'s really stressed about it.

P.P.S. If I were renovating the basement bathrooms, I'd make a special place where people could go and forget their problems.

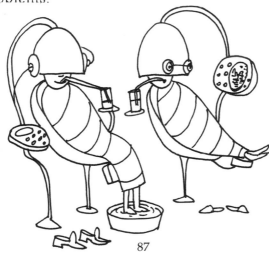

From My Bath Room

FLORENCE WATERS
4 BUBBLE STREET
BATH, ENGLAND

August 23

Gil
Administrative *Asset*
c/o Geyser Creek Middle School
Geyser Creek, Missouri USA

Dear Gil,

Dumb? Gil, you're one of the smartest people I know! Your ideas regarding the bathrooms are pure genius.

Of course I'm still coming for the SPA conference. I wouldn't miss it for the world.

But good gravy, there seems to be a lot of stress in Geyser Creek these days. We must do something about that—and those bathrooms, too. Let's work together on this, shall we?

Take a picture of the graffiti and send it to me. But don't send the photos of your bathrooms to my Bath room. This city is crawling with police officers who keep pestering me with a lot of silly questions. So I'm heading to Pompeii, Italy, to take a nice mud bath. Send the photos to me in Pompeii, general delivery.

And *please* don't worry. The only thing we have to stress about is stress itself!

Yours in Bath (but not for long), Florence

P.S. I'll handle Wally's speech. Can't Pearl cut his hair?

88

Gil
Summer Intern

August 26

To Florence Waters
c/o General Delivery
Pompeii, Italy

Dear Florence,

Thanks for your nice letter.

Here are some pictures of the bathroom graffiti.

If you have any ideas about how to get the graffiti off, please let me know.

I gotta dash. There's something going on behind school. The sheriff's here!

Gil

✷THE GEYSER CREEK GAZETTE✷

Our motto: "We have a nose for news!"

Friday, August 26 | **Late Edition** | **50 cents**

Human Bones Discovered by Middle School Students
Mander-Eel case closed

By Tad Poll, Investigative Reporter-in-Training
(with editorial assistance from Annette Trap)

I can't believe what my friends just found! *[Tad: Put yourself in the background of news stories. –A. T.]* Two savvy 12-year-old girls accidentally cracked the case of the summer. *[Good! –A. T.]*

While investigating the alleged mole damage in their teacher's garden earlier today, two summer school students named Lily and Paddy found human bones buried in the dirt.

"A preliminary analysis suggests the bones are part of the skeletal remains of a man and a woman," said Lily. "We need to study the bones to determine their age and identity."

Not necessary, said authorities. According to investigator Lieut. Sting Ray, the girls discovered the remains of the late Sally Mander and Delbert "Dee" Eel, who escaped from jail two months ago.

"Once again these kids have cracked the case and saved the day," said Ray.

With the discovery of Eel's and Mander's remains, Sheriff Mack Rell declared the case of

Students find bones in garden.

the villainous duo closed.

"Everybody can get back to their regular lives," said Rell. "Well, I mean, those of us who are regular. Hope you feel better soon, Wally!"

It's nice to know our law enforcement officials are able to joke around. Meanwhile, some locals (including this reporter) feel a bit unsatisfied with the way this story ended. We still don't know why Sally and Dee came to town in the first place, or how they escaped from jail. *[Tad, the case is closed. End of story. –A. T.]*

Locals Remember Sally Mander and Dee Eel

Pearl gave Dee and Sally haircuts the day before their escape.

The late Sally Mander and Delbert "Dee" Eel will be remembered for their decades-long scam, which effectively robbed local residents of free water.

But some locals remember a kinder, gentler side of the convicts.

"They were real sweet when I trimmed their hair," said hairstylist Pearl O. Ster, who has a contract with Geyser Creek County to provide regular haircuts for inmates at the jail.

"I was over there the day before they escaped," said Ster. "They wanted to hear all about my jazzy new beauty treatments. They said they'd never seen me looking so young. Bless their poor dead hearts."

Ster said both Mander and Eel had fine but thinning hair.

"I've still got a bag of their hair clippings," Ster said. "I was saving it to make wigs for them."

Cafe Florence to Close after SPA Conference
Russ scheduled for surgery

By Tad Poll, Investigative Reporter-in-Training
(with editorial assistance from Annette Trap)

Cafe Florence, conceived as a labor of love by newlyweds Chef Angelo and Angel Fisch, will close its doors after Chef Angelo prepares and serves a final meal for the Society of Principals and Administrators (SPA) conference next Wednesday.

Chef Angelo acknowledged his role in the mishaps that led to the restaurant's failure.

"Everything it is all my big knucklyhead mistake," Chef Angelo said.

"You're darn tootin' it's his fault," Fisch said through her attorney, Barry Cuda.

Due to an ordering mistake, the menu at Cafe Florence has been limited to dishes that can be prepared with chicken, chocolate and eggs.

"Plus, I have the few spices," said Chef Angelo, who served spicy chocolate chicken omelets for breakfast yesterday.

"You coulda gagged a maggot with that slop," said Sheriff Mack Rell.

Out of desperation, Geyser Creek Middle School Principal Walter Russ has agreed to let Chef Angelo prepare the SPA banquet.

"What have I got to lose?" Russ said in a handwritten press release he slid to reporters under the faculty restroom door. "The whole conference is going to be a big flop anyway."

Russ fired renowned designer Florence Waters, whom he'd enlisted to renovate the bathrooms in the school basement in time for

Chef Angelo will leave Geyser Creek next week.

the SPA conference. Now he's relying on his administrative assistant, 12-year-old Gil, to oversee the bathroom project.

"I guess I'm number two in command," Gil said. "So to speak."

Speaking of number two *[Tad! –A. T.]*, Gladys Ownleepoup, MD, of Springfield made a personal visit to Geyser Creek Middle School yesterday to check on Russ.

"His condition is very serious," said Dr. Ownleepoup, who specializes in intestinal disorders. "I've scheduled him for surgery on August 31."

Ownleepoup said that unless Russ "can take care of the matter himself," he will miss the SPA conference.

"This is certainly no laughing matter," said Ownleepoup, winner of last year's Colin Bowell Award for intestinal fortitude.

Dr. Gladys Ownleepoup makes a "school call" to visit Principal Walter Russ.

Did y'all know?

RIP is Latin for *Requiescat in pace*, which means: "May he/she rest in peace."

IDEA BOX

Here's today's best idea submitted to the idea box.

As compiled by Shelly, Mayor I. B. Newt's summer intern

MY IDEA IS: Now that Sally and Dee are dead and gone, let's celebrate by having a big old party with lots of good food. That's what I'd like Geyser Creek to be known for: good old-fashioned cooking. None of this new-fangled stuff that Chef Angelo's been coming up with. No offense, buddy! —Sheriff Mack Rell

Annette Trap Invited to Speak at Editors' Workshop

By Tad Poll, Investigative Reporter-in-Training
(with editorial assistance from Annette Trap)

Trap may take trip.

Annette Trap, editor of the *Gazette*, has been invited to speak at the National Editors Workshop Seminar (NEWS) in St. Louis next week.

Trap said she hadn't decided whether to accept the invitation.

"I don't want publication of the *Gazette* to be interrupted," she said. "I'll go if I can find someone to put one edition of the paper to bed without me."

"Putting a paper to bed" is an expression journalists use to describe the process of preparing a newspaper for publication.

"I have someone in mind," said Trap. "I just want him to get a little more experience."

[Nice job on this story, Tad. Can you guess whom I'm going to ask to take my place while I'm gone? You! –A. T.]

Desperately Seeking Information

Does *anyone* know anything about the ancient history of Geyser Creek, or how the Jawlseedat Mountain got its name?

Please contact Minnie O. at the His, Hers, and Theirs-torical Society.

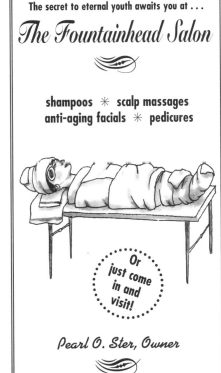

Lily Pad's
Private Investigations, Etc.
c/o **Geyser Creek Middle School**
Geyser Creek, Missouri

Founders and Agents: Lily and Paddy
His, Hers, and Theirs-torical Research: Minnie O.
Investigative Research: Tad Poll
Director of Ideas: Shelly

Hand Delivered

August 26

Pearl O. Ster
The Fountainhead Salon
104 Main Street
Geyser Creek, Missouri

Dear Pearl,

We know this sounds weird, but can we have those hair clippings you saved from Sally's and Dee's last haircuts? We'd like to run DNA tests on them.

Sorry so rushed. We're sorta in a hurry!

Lily   Paddy

The Fountainhead Salon

Where Every Day Is a Good Hair Day

104 Main Street
Geyser Creek, Missouri

Delivered by Manicured Hand

August 26

Lily and Paddy,

Sure, girls! Come on over. Hope you have time to sit a
spell and visit with me.

You kids sure seem stressed out this summer.

Pearl

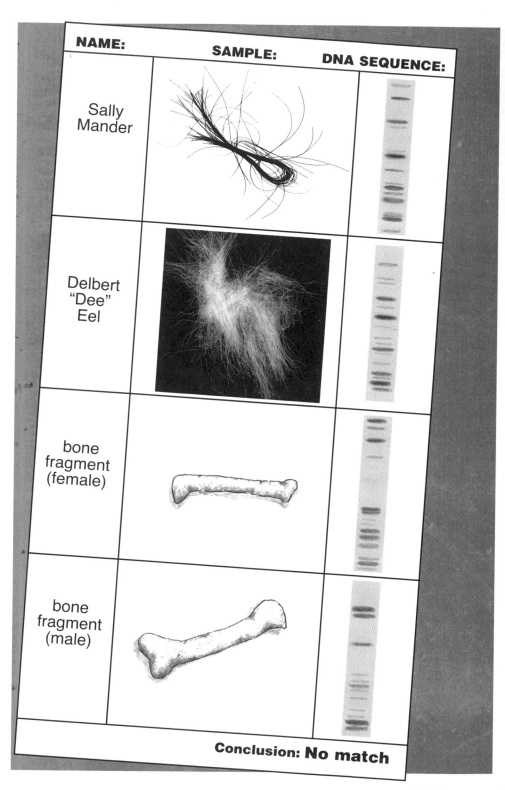

NAME:	SAMPLE:	DNA SEQUENCE:
Sally Mander		
Delbert "Dee" Eel		
bone fragment (female)		
bone fragment (male)		

Conclusion: **No match**

Lily Pad's
Private Investigations, Etc.
c/o Geyser Creek Middle School
Geyser Creek, Missouri

Founders and Agents: Lily and Paddy
His, Hers, and Theirs-torical Research: Minnie O.
Investigative Research: Tad Poll
Director of Ideas: Shelly

August 26

Sheriff Mack Rell
Geyser Creek Sheriff's
Office
Geyser Creek, Missouri

Sting,
I don't have any alacritters.
Will you talk to the kids?
Thanks, pal.
Mack

Sheriff,

REQUEST FOR INTERVIEW

Now that the Mander and Eel case is closed, we are officially requesting permission to interview you or Sting Ray.

Remember, you promised you'd give us the straight poop when the investigation was over.

Please respond with alacrity.

Agent Lily   Agent Paddy

INTERVIEW WITH STING RAY
BY LILY AND PADDY

TRANSCRIPT

Lily: We want to ask you a few questions about the Mander and Eel case. We're concerned because the DNA from their hair samples doesn't match the DNA of the bones we found in Mr. N.'s garden.

Paddy: This leads us to conclude that Sally and Dee might still be alive.

Sting Ray: Of course Sally and Dee are still alive. But that's old news, girls. I've been in touch with your friend at Interpol.

Lily: Who?

Sting Ray: Hugh Dunnit. I'm working with him on a case involving an international antiquities looter.

Lily and Paddy: So are we!

Sting Ray: I'm about to crack this thing wide open.

Lily: You are?

Sting Ray: Yep. The looter's a friend of yours.

Paddy: Who?

Sting Ray: Here's her picture.

Lily (laughing): But that's Florence. She's no thief.

Sting Ray: Wanna bet?

Paddy: You don't mean Florence is stealing priceless pieces of history and selling them over the Internet? She would *never* do something like that.

Sting Ray: Oh, wouldn't she? Not only is Waters an international thief, she's got Sally Mander and Dee Eel working for her, hiding her stash of stolen goods right here in Geyser Creek.

Paddy: I don't believe you.

Lily: And I don't believe Hugh Dunnit believes you.

Sting Ray: He didn't at first. Then he started thinking about it. A woman who travels the world, often in disguise. Never accepts payment for her services. Has no visible means of support.

Lily: That's circumstantial evidence. Do you have any proof?

Sting Ray: The facts don't lie, girls. Don't worry. This will all be sorted out when she comes for the SPA conference.

Paddy: What do you mean?

Lily: What do you have there?

Sting Ray: An arrest warrant. For Florence Waters.

WANTED!

FLORENCE WATERS
as last seen in Bath, England

On Charges of Stealing Priceless Antiquities

Waters as seen in some of her various disguises:

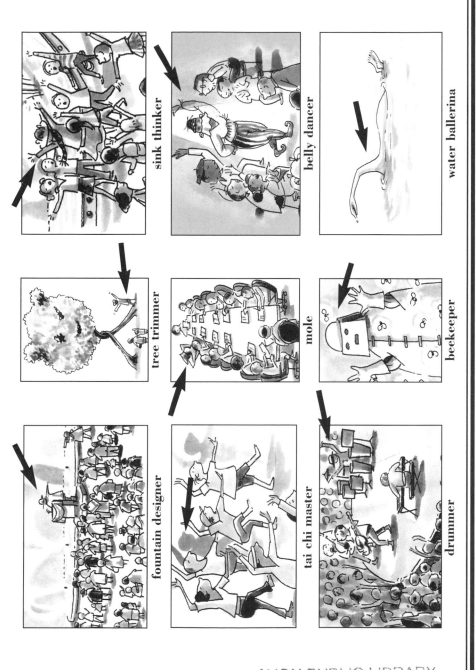

sink thinker

belly dancer

water ballerina

tree trimmer

mole

beekeeper

fountain designer

tai chi master

drummer

Lily Pad's
Private Investigations, Etc.
c/o Geyser Creek Middle School
Geyser Creek, Missouri

Founders and Agents: Lily and Paddy
His, Hers, and Theirs-torical Research: Minnie O.
Investigative Research: Tad Poll
Director of Ideas: Shelly

FAX

DATE: August 26
TO: Mr. Hugh Dunnit
　　　　Director of Investigations, Interpol
FR: Agents Lily and Paddy
RE: Urgent matter

URGENT! OFFICIAL REPORT FROM GEYSER CREEK

We hardly know where to begin. So much has happened since our last report.

We discovered some human bones in the garden behind school. It's a long story, but local authorities originally said the bones were from the skeletal remains of Sally Mander and Dee Eel, some crafty cons who escaped from jail in June.

We ran DNA tests on the bones and hair samples from Mander and Eel. They didn't match. The bones and hair samples don't share the same DNA. So we kept digging and found even more bones. Lots of them! They're ancient! And there's other stuff buried around school, too, like old pottery and tools.

But here's the crazy thing: Sting Ray, our local investigator, is convinced Florence Waters is the international antiquities looter.

We hope you agree with us that Sting's assessment of the situation is completely ridiculous. We will continue to help you bring this case to justice and catch the international looters, whoever they may be.

Agent Lily   Agent Paddy

P.S. Sorry we haven't gotten our CVs to you yet. We've been really busy.

(i)NTERPOL

International Criminal Police Organization

FAX

DATE: 26 August
TO: Lily and Paddy
Students, Geyser Creek Middle School
FR: Hugh Dunnit
RE: The truth

Lily and Paddy:

You've been busy all right—making *me* look ridiculous.

Sting Ray told me how old you are. No wonder you were reluctant to provide your CVs.

For your information, Lieut. Ray's analysis of the facts appears to be correct. The skeletal remains buried near your school are indeed ancient. Florence likely placed them there, along with other priceless antiquities, the last time she was in Geyser Creek. She's using a site under your school to hide her stolen goods.

It's an ingenious foil, but of course we would expect nothing less from Florence Waters. (No wonder she asked me to contact you. She wanted to throw me off *her* trail.)

I'm currently awaiting a court order that will allow me to subpoena records from several online auction houses. This will give us the evidence we need to charge Florence Waters with international looting. We'll arrest her when she arrives in Geyser Creek for the SPA conference.

We've set the trap. Now to catch the old mole.

Hugh Dunnit
Hugh Dunnit

P.S. No need to send your CVs. You are officially dismissed from this case—and any future cases with Interpol.

Lily Pad's
Private Investigations, Etc.
c/o Geyser Creek Middle School
Geyser Creek, Missouri

Founders and Agents: Lily and Paddy
His, Hers, and Theirs-torical Research: Minnie O.
Investigative Research: Tad Poll
Director of Ideas: Shelly

OVERNIGHT MAIL—URGENT!

August 26

Florence Waters
Our <u>Endangered</u> Friend
4 Bubble Street
Bath, England

Dear Florence,

Oh.
My.
GOSH!

Please don't come to Geyser Creek. It's a long complicated story, but until we get this sorted out, DON'T COME HERE! We don't want you to be arrested for something you didn't do.

Love,

Lily   Paddy

P.S. You're not an international antiquities looter, are you, Florence?

Hotel Pompeii
Via della Fortuna
Pompeii, Italy

Our hotel is conveniently located near Pompeii's central baths, which were destroyed in AD 79 with the eruption of Mt. Vesuvius, a powerful volcano that buried this ancient city and its unlucky residents.

August 27

Mr. Sam N.'s Summer School Class
Geyser Creek Middle School
Geyser Creek, Missouri USA

Dear Friends,

Just a quick note to say I'll be incommunicado until I arrive in Geyser Creek on the 30th. I have urgent business here with friends in the underground economy. We're meeting at a secret location, where mail delivery is impossible.

Nothing to be concerned about. Just business as usual.

See you the day after tomorrow!

*Semper in media res,**

P.S. to Lily and Paddy: Did you ever solve the Case of the Dirty Bathrooms? (That's a gentle hint that I think Gil could use your assistance, and perhaps you could use *his* help, too.)

*That's Latin for "Always in the middle of things."

Lily Pad's

Private Investigations, Etc.

c/o Geyser Creek Middle School

Geyser Creek, Missouri

Founders and Agents: Lily and Paddy
His, Hers, and Theirs-torical Research: Minnie O.
Investigative Research: Tad Poll
Director of Ideas: Shelly

Delivered in Person

August 29

Gil,

We're so sorry we haven't helped you with the bathrooms.

We'll start by doing a chemical analysis of the dirt on the walls. That'll tell us what kind of cleaner we need. Okay?

Lily   Paddy

P.S. Will you please join our PI firm? We need you!

FROM THE DESK OF GIL
Administrative Assistant to Principal Walter Russ
Geyser Creek Middle School   Geyser Creek, Missouri

Gil
Summer Intern

August 29

Lily and Paddy,

Yes and yes!

Meet me in the basement bathrooms. I'll be
the one covered in dirt.

Gil

To: Principal Russ
Fr: Gil
Re: The bathrooms
Date: August 30

I've found a company that can fix up the basement
bathrooms in time for the SPA conference tomorrow.
It's called Lily Pad's Private Investigations, Etc. The
crew's working on the job right now. The restored
bathrooms will be *very* traditional.

Also, because Fisher Cutbait is on vacation, I've
made an appointment for you to get a haircut at
6:30 tonight at Pearl's shop.

I'll stand outside the restroom door while you write
your response.

August 30

Ms. Trap,

A reliable source tells me that Principal Russ will be emerging from the faculty restroom tonight to get his hair cut at Pearl's.

Want me to cover it? I think it'll be an exclusive.

Tad Poll

P.S. I'd really like to keep digging into the Mander and Eel case, too, if that's okay.

★THE GEYSER CREEK GAZETTE★

"We have a nose for news!"

Annette Trap, Editor

To: Tad Poll
Fr: Annette Trap
Re: The next issue
Date: August 30

Yes, please cover Wally's haircut. You can include it in tomorrow's edition, which you'll be putting to bed yourself.

Don't worry. The issue's almost done. You just need to take a few photos and write a story or two. I know you can do it.

See you tomorrow afternoon when I get back from the NEWS conference.

A. Trap

P.S. Here's the mock-up for tomorrow's paper. As you can see, there's no room for another Sally and Dee story. Sorry, Tad, but I just don't think there's anything more to say on that case. Besides, the news about Florence is *much* bigger—and sadder. (I've written most of the story, thanks to a tip from Sting Ray. You'll just have to fill in the blanks.)

☀THE GEYSER CREEK GAZETTE☀

Our motto: "We have a nose for news!"

Wednesday, August 31 | **Late Edition** | **50 cents**

* * * MOCK-UP * * *

FLORENCE WATERS ARRESTED IN GEYSER CREEK!

Internationally famous fountain designer Florence Waters, who befriended students at Geyser Creek Middle School with her charm and purported generosity, was arrested last night at approximately _____ p.m. She was charged with antiquities looting.

Before the arrest, investigator Lieut. Sting Ray told the *Gazette* he was as disappointed as anyone to learn of Waters's true motives in Geyser Creek.

"Our mistake was believing that someone would do all the nice things Florence Waters did for this town for free," Ray said. "We should've suspected she had an ulterior motive: money."

At the time of her arrest, Waters appeared _____. *[Tad, give a good description here of her physical/mental state.]*

[Tad: You'll have to take this photo and finish the story.]

Waters will be held at _____*[where]* until her preliminary hearing on _____*[date]*. She is expected to plead _____*[guilty/not guilty]*.

Cafe Florence to Close

Chef Angelo will leave Geyser Creek—alone.

After he serves a banquet dinner to the Society of Principals and Administrators tonight, Chef Angelo will close the doors to Cafe Florence for the last time.

Asked to describe his plans for the future, Angelo said: "My future? *Pfffftt.* It's nothing. Me, the big failure. I ruin the marriage. I ruin my Angel's business. I stink up the whole town with bad egg smelly. What can I to do but move back to Italy and live my life in only sadness?"

Principal Walter Russ Gets Presurgery Haircut

[Tad: You'll have to take this photo and finish the story.]

Principals and Administrators Arrive for SPA Conference

[Tad, please write this story. Include news of Wally's surgery.]

And of course, if there's breaking news, you'll have to cover that, too. Good luck, Tad!

A. Trap

August 30 TUESDAY

9:00	
9:30	
10:00	
10:30	*relax*
11:00	
11:30	
12:00	*lunch*
12:30	
1:00	
1:30	
2:00	*nap*
2:30	
3:00	
3:30	
4:00	
4:30	
5:30	*CeCe Salt (color/perm)*
6:00	
6:30	*Wally (haircut)*
7:00	
7:30	
8:00	

Hiya, Pearl.

Hawaii's real pretty, but it ain't Geyser Creek. See ya when I get back.

Fisher Cutbait

Pearl
c/o The Fountainhead Salon
104 Main Street
Geyser Creek, Missouri

BROAD STINGRAY (Dasyatis lata): Stingrays are innocent-looking but highly dangerous creatures. You can tell that you're near stingrays by the presence of large craters and pits in the sand, created by rays as they excavate for buried prey.

3:30	
4:00	
4:30	
5:30	
6:00	
6:30	
7:00	
7:30	
8:00	

TRANSCRIPT

Tad Poll: Hi, Pearl. Mind if I interview Principal Russ while you're cutting his hair?

Pearl: I don't mind if Wally and Gil here don't mind.

Gil: Fine with me.

Walter Russ: I guess it's okay.

Tad Poll: Thanks. So, Mr. Russ, are you excited about the big SPA conference tomorrow?

Walter Russ: I won't be participating. I'll be in surgery.

Pearl: For that blocked bowel of yours? My uncle John had the same problem. Really his name was Frank, but we called him John because he was always in the john. Problem was he couldn't go, just like you, Wally. So he went to the hospital and they hooked him up to a big machine and pumped it right out of him. Boy-man-howdy, what a mess that must've been.

Walter Russ: I'd rather not talk about it.

Pearl: About the pump? Well, that's what they have to use when you're—

[SOUND OF DOOR OPENING/CLOSING; ENTER FLORENCE WATERS]

Florence Waters: Hello, hello? Anybody home?

Tad Poll: Florence! You're here! Quick, you've got to hide because—

Florence Waters: Of course I'm here. Pearl, can you squeeze me in for a shampoo and a cut?

Pearl: Sure, honey pie. Have a seat. I'll get to you after I finish Wally.

Walter Russ: Hello, Ms. Waters.

Florence Waters: Wally! Lovely to see you. But good heavens, you look awful. Didn't you eat those prunes I sent?

[SOUND OF DOOR OPENING/CLOSING; ENTER MACK RELL AND STING RAY]

118

Mack Rell: Hold it right there, Waters.

Florence Waters: Macky! Sting! Good to see you again, boys.

Sting Ray: Cut the cute stuff, Florence. We're onto your game.

Florence Waters: My game? Which game would that be? My tennis game isn't what it used to be. And my croquet game is—

Sting Ray: Let's cuff her.

Tad Poll: You can't do that to Florence!

Sting Ray: Watch me.

Florence Waters: Oh my. How exciting! I'm being arrested. I wonder why.

Sting Ray: You know why, Waters. Stealing rare antiquities and selling them online.

[SOUND OF DOOR OPENING/CLOSING; ENTER LILY, PADDY, SHELLY, AND MINNIE O.]

Lily: Not so fast, Sting.

Sting Ray: What's this?

Paddy: You heard her. Drop the handcuffs, Sting. You're under arrest.

Mack Rell: Arrest? What've you got there, girls?

Minnie O.: A citizen's arrest. Signed by Judge Anne Chovey.

Lily: C'mon, Sting. She's expecting you in her chambers now.

Sting Ray: I don't know what you're talking about.

Sally Mander (her head emerging from a panel in the floor): Can it, Sting.

Delbert "Dee" Eel (his head emerging from a nearby floor panel): It's time to come clean, old Stinger.

Tad Poll: Sally! Dee! You're alive!

Sally Mander: Of course we're alive—thanks to the garden your teacher planted. We've been living off it all summer.

Shelly: So it wasn't moles eating Mr. N.'s garden after all.

Delbert "Dee" Eel: The only mole in town is standing right there.

Sting Ray: I have no idea why you're pointing at me.

Sally Mander: Oh, tell it to the judge, Sting. These kids know you let us out of jail so we could dig for the antiquities *you* were selling online.

Delbert "Dee" Eel: Yeah, but we got tired of doing your dirty work, Stinger. Besides, we finally found what we were looking for—and the reason we moved to this crummy town in the first place.

Tad Poll: What? Why?

Liz Ard (her head emerging from a toilet): The Fountain of Youth!

Paddy: Liz! How'd you get out of jail?

Liz Ard: Down the toilet, of course. You think I was going to let my sister beat me out of my share of the Fountain of Youth again? Not a chance.

Lily: The Fountain of Youth is in Geyser Creek? I can't wait to tell Hugh Dunnit about this.

[SOUND OF DOOR OPENING/CLOSING; ENTER HUGH DUNNIT]

Hugh Dunnit: And I can't wait to hear it. I've got some news myself.

Florence Waters: Hugh! Lovely to see you. Didn't I tell you my friends were fabulous investigators?

Hugh Dunnit: I've never seen anything like it. These kids cracked a case that had agents around the world stumped.

Florence Waters: This demands a celebration—to all of our mysteries solved!

Minnie O.: Not all of them. We still don't know how the Jawlseedat Mountain got its name.

[SOUND OF EXPLOSION OUTSIDE]

Gil: What the heck was that?

Pearl: Look out the window. Did y'all see that?

Minnie O.: Pearl, what did you just say?

Pearl: I said, Did you all see that?

Minnie O.: No. You said, "Did y'all see that?"

Paddy: Why are you smiling, Minnie?

Minnie O.: Say it fast.

Paddy: Did y'all see that?

Minnie O.: Faster.

Lily: Did y'all see that.

Minnie O.: Even faster. Like it's one word.

Shelly: Did y'all see that? Didy'allseethat.

Pearl: For pity's sake, girls. Be quiet and look out the window. The whole ding-dang Jawlseedat Mountain's on fire.

Lily: Don't worry, Pearl. It's not on fire. And I don't think it's a mountain.

Minnie O.: But I think I know how Jawlseedat Mountain got its name.

Paddy: I think I know who the real antiquities looter is.

Gil: I think I know why those basement bathrooms were always so dirty.

Shelly: I think I know how we can attract tourists to Geyser Creek.

Walter Russ: I think I have to go to the bathroom.

Pearl: What about your haircut?

Walter Russ: No time for that. I've . . . GOTTA GO.

Florence Waters: Oh, Wally, that's wonderful news! Tad, I think you've got a breaking story here.

Tad Poll: No kidding! Everybody hold still while I take a picture.

[SOUND OF CAMERA FLASH]

✳ THE GEYSER CREEK GAZETTE ✳

Motto: "With apologies to Annette Trap."

50 cents   Wednesday, August 31

Jawlseedat ~~Mountain~~ Volcano Erupts! Did y'all see that?

By Tad Poll, Investigative Reporter-in-Training
(without the benefit of editorial assistance from Annette Trap)

Well, get this: It turns out the Jawlseedat Mountain is a volcano, as evidenced by its eruption last night. We should've known. Geysers are almost always located near areas of high volcanic activity.

We had other hints that the mountain was really a volcano. The unpleasant odor lingering around town lately wasn't caused by hard-boiled eggs (Sorry, Chef Angelo!) but by the release of sulphur gas—a sign that magma has risen in a dormant volcano and an eruption might be dangerously close.

But perhaps the biggest clue of all was the name of the mountain, as summer researcher Minnie O. discovered.

"When the volcano erupted and Pearl said, 'Did y'all see that?' I realized the mountain was probably named by early settlers who saw the volcano erupt," said Minnie O., who has spent the summer studying Geyser Creek's ancient history.

The Jawlseedat Mountain erupted last night, proving it's a volcano.

Luckily, no one was hurt in the volcanic eruption, except the no-good stinkers who emerged from the bowels of Pearl O. Ster's shop shortly before the dramatic eruption, and the dirty rotten mole behind it all. (See story below.)

Sting Stung!
Lily and Paddy make citizen's arrest on Sting Ray

By Tad Poll, Investigative Reporter-in-Training

Lieut. Sting Ray was charged last night with antiquities looting, conspiracy, fraud and illegally releasing Sally Mander and Delbert "Dee" Eel from Geyser Creek County Jail.

"Sally and Dee had a really easy escape," explained Lily of Lily Pad's Private Investigations, Etc. "Sting let them out so they could work for him in his antiquities-looting business."

Like many criminals, Sting tried to pin his evildoing on others.

(Continued on page 2, column 1)

DNA from saliva on envelopes was used as evidence in Sting's arrest.

STING (Continued from page 1, column 1)

I also hope y with or witho

My sister, Liz Ard, had nothing to do with this.
—Sally Mander

Sting Ray
Sting Ray

Sting's signature gave him away, students say.

"First, he forged that jail letter from Sally Mander as a red herring," said Paddy, who provided Interpol authorities with an analysis of Ray's handwriting. The *S* in Sting Ray's signature matched the *S* in the note found in Sally Mander's jail cell.

"Sting said the letter was forged by Liz Ard, but it was actually written by him," said Lily, who also matched the DNA of the saliva on the back of the jail envelope with DNA from an envelope Ray had sent Lily Pad's Private Investigations, Etc.

"If he licked it, he'll be convicted," predicted Paddy.

According to Lily and Paddy, Ray tried to divert their investigation by hinting that Sheriff Mack Rell was a mole. Finally, when Ray found out the students were working with Interpol to crack the antiquities-looting case, he contacted Hugh Dunnit, director of investigations for Interpol, and tried to convince Dunnit that Florence Waters was the looter.

"As if," said Lily.

The student-run detective agency used forensic science and good old-fashioned sleuthing to sting Ray. They credited a postcard from Fisher Cutbait with helping them crack Ray's online alias, *Dasyatislata*.

"*Dasyatis lata* is Latin for 'stingray,' " said Lily.

Dunnit arrived in Geyser Creek last night with documents seized from online auction houses that linked Ray's computer at the sheriff's office with the source of the online antiquities sales.

Confronted with the overwhelming evidence, Ray came clean. He confessed to the crimes and explained how he had freed Mander and Eel from jail on the condition they retrieve priceless antiquities buried under Geyser Creek Middle School.

A full report of the case will be published in tomorrow's edition of the *Gazette*.

Sally Mander, Dee Eel, Liz Ard were also caught and rebooked.

Chef Angelo Discovers *Mole*

By Tad Poll, Investigative Reporter-in-Training

Okay, so there weren't moles in the summer school garden. There *was* a mole at the sheriff's office.

And now Chef Angelo says that thanks to last night's volcanic eruption, he's discovered a delicious chicken dish called *mole* (pronounced *moh-LAY*) that he plans to serve at the Society of Principals and Administrators (SPA) banquet tonight.

"I was cooking the little chicken and stirring a chocolate sauce when everything it starts shaking and rumbling," explained Chef Angelo. "Before I know what is happening, my spices they fall from shelf into sauce and then spicy sauce splash on chicken. I think, *Oh no!* Then I think, *Maybe I should to taste this.* And what do I to discover? It is *magnifico!*"

Chef Angelo hopes his chicken *mole* will impress his almost-ex-wife, Angel Fisch.

"I must to have my Angel try the chicken *mole*," Chef Angelo said.

Goldie Fisch agreed to deliver a sample of mole to her sister, Angel, in Springfield.

"I have to go to Springfield anyway for a doctor's appointment," said Goldie.

Lava Story Behind Dirty *Lavatories*

By Tad Poll, Investigative Reporter-in-Training

Gil leads fellow classmates in excavation of middle school bathrooms.

This is breaking news, and I don't really have all the details yet.

But Gil and the others tell me that when they started renovating the basement bathrooms yesterday, they found what appears to be ancient baths.

"I thought they were just dirty, but it turns out the bathrooms were covered in volcanic ash," said Gil, who led last night's all-night excavation project.

More on this in the next edition of the *Gazette*. For now, let's just say it seems there's a *lava* story behind our dirty *lavatories*.

Florence Waters Arrives in Geyser Creek *Well* Rested, Not *Ar*rested

By Tad Poll, Investigative Reporter-in-Training

Florence Waters arrived in Geyser Creek last night, well rested after her summer vacation in England and Italy.

A class of summer school students from Geyser Creek Middle School thwarted Lieut. Sting Ray's plan to arrest Waters upon her arrival in town.

"I would've been up a creek without Paddy, Lily and the rest of the brilliant children in this town," Waters gushed.

IDEA BOX

Here's today's best idea submitted to the idea box.

As compiled by Shelly, Mayor I. B. Newt's summer intern

MY IDEA IS: My classmates and I have a *spa*ctacular idea for turning Geyser Creek into a fantabulous tourist destination! Come to the SPA conference and we'll show you what we mean.
— Shelly

I'm also working on breaking stories about:

● the alleged discovery of the Fountain of Youth in Geyser Creek

● the arrival of 300 principals and administrators in town for the SPA conference

● Principal Walter Russ's full recovery from his, uh, you know, condition

---

Sorry this is so sloppy, folks. I'm doing the best I can! Tad Poll

August 31

TODAY'S ASSIGNMENTS:

Tad: Cover excavation, investigation, and arrival of SPA guests for the _Gazette_; design SPA program

Shelly: _Call special session of mayor's tourism task force; milk cows_

Minnie O.: Finish writing report on GC's ancient history; dry loofah gourds

Gil: Oversee restoration project; get eggs and chocolate from Chef Angelo

Lily & Paddy: Conclude interrogations of Mander, Eel, Ard, and Ray; prepare mud baths

Mr. N.: Harvest summer garden

Meet in basement bathrooms at 10 a.m. **EVERYONE!**

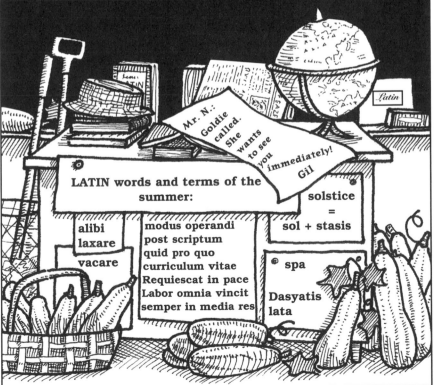

Mr. N.:
Goldie called. She wants to see you immediately!
Gil

LATIN words and terms of the summer:

solstice
=
sol + stasis

alibi
laxare
vacare

modus operandi
post scriptum
quid pro quo
curriculum vitae
Requiescat in pace
Labor omnia vincit
semper in media res

spa

Dasyatis
lata

Welcome
Society of Principals and Administrators

Please proceed to the
Geyser Creek Middle School

BATHROOMS

located in the
school basement
for a
speech
by
~~Principal Walter Russ~~

Florence Waters

Doctor of Bathology
Professor of *Gee*ology
Road Scholar
Rebel without a Pause
President of Flowing Waters Fountains, Etc.
and
Founder of
Fabulous Bathrooms
for Middle Schools,
Unlimited
!

**After the speech, you are cordially invited
to enjoy our:**

thermal springs
Jawlseedat mud baths
fresh milk baths
chocolate baths
salt scrubs with loofah
pumice pedicures & foot massages

cucumber eye treatments
egg-white facials
summer school whirlpools
destress-your-tresses scalp massages
warm lava wraps

Age-reversing **Stress-reducing** **Really reeeeelaxing**

Don't miss the SPA banquet, tonight at Cafe Florence!

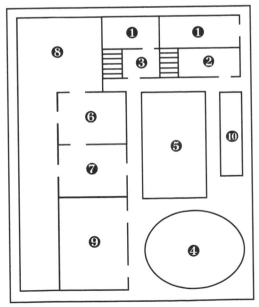

❶ apodyterium
(changing room)
❷ tepidarium
(warm room)
❸ caldarium
(hot room)
❹ frigidarium
(cold room)
❺ natatio
(swimming pool)
❻ library
❼ gymnasium
❽ gardens
❾ auditorium
❿ art gallery

Map of Basement Bathrooms

☆ THE GEYSER CREEK GAZETTE ☆

Our motto: "We have a nose for news!"

| Wednesday, August 31 | Late Edition | 50 cents |

Middle School Bathrooms: Privy Portals to the Past

By Tad Poll, Investigative Reporter-in-Training

Basement bathrooms confirm Geyser Creek's *geeo*logical past as an ancient spa town.

Who would've guessed the filthy bathrooms in the Geyser Creek Middle School basement are archaeological treasures?

Or that the school was constructed on top of ancient baths buried by a volcanic eruption? Or that Ponce de León, the Spanish explorer, believed that the Fountain of Youth was located somewhere in Geyser Creek?

It's all true, said Rob R. Dukky, a world-renowned authority on ancient baths who traveled to Geyser Creek at the request of Florence Waters.

"Florence showed me photos of the school bathrooms taken by a student," Dukky said. "After examining the so-called graffiti, as well as the subterranean rooms under the bathrooms, it's clear to me that this site has been used by multiple civilizations as a sacred and secular communal bathing area."

Translation? The bathrooms in the Geyser Creek Middle School basement are totally cool bathrooms where people have been bathing and

swimming for thousands of years!

Minnie O., summer intern at the Geyser Creek His, Hers and Theirs-torical Society, said the discovery of ancient baths under the school, along with the dramatic eruption of the Jawlseedat Mountain, reveals valuable information about our town's ancient history.

"Geyser Creek's history began millions of years ago with the eruption of Mt. Jawlseedat," said Minnie O. "The eruption deposited volcanic ash on our town, which Paleoindians used for mud baths. That eruption, or a later one, also left a fissure in the earth through which groundwater reaches the hot magma at 4,000 feet and then resurfaces as our local geyser."

The drawings on the bathroom walls suggest that early settlers lived in harmony with their surroundings, according to Minnie O. "Our ancestors had great respect for the volcano, the local waters and the summer solstice, which they marked with a stone calendar, much

(Continued on page 2, column 2)

SPA Conferees Enjoy Spa Spree

By Tad Poll, Investigative Reporter-in-Training

The Society of Principals and Administrators (SPA) conference was an unexpected success, said Geyser Creek Middle School Principal Walter Russ.

Russ was able to attend the conference after his medical condition was remedied when he witnessed the volcanic eruption last night.

"It sorta got things moving," said Russ with a shrug.

Russ welcomed the visiting principals and administrators and led them on a tour of the school. He then turned the conference over to Florence Waters, who delivered the presentation on Russ's new management philosophy. (See sidebar on page 3.)

After the presentation SPA conferees enjoyed the ancient baths discovered beneath the middle school basement. Because of the volcanic soil, the spa waters contain both sulfur and bicarbonate, producing an almost intoxicating effect for soakers. Others preferred the chocolate baths, milk baths and egg-white facials prepared by Mr. Sam N.'s summer school class. Still other principals and administrators enjoyed working out in the ancient gymnasium.

So far students have uncovered an art gallery, a library, an auditorium, a gymnasium, a garden area and various swimming and bathing pools in the baths beneath the school basement.

The SPA conference concluded with a banquet at Cafe Florence, where Chef Angelo served chicken *mole,* a native Mexican dish that combines chicken with a dark spicy chocolate sauce.

Angel Fisch was so impressed by her husband's cooking that she used the proceeds from the recent sale of her wedding ring to buy ingredients to make whole-grain tortillas and breads, which she served alongside the chicken *mole* and summer-school garden vegetables.

"My wife she is the brilliant Angel," said Chef Angelo, who called the banquet fare an example of Cafe Florence's new spa cuisine.

School principals and administrators enjoy ancient baths discovered in middle school basement.

Chef Angelo and Angel Fisch serve spa cuisine at banquet.

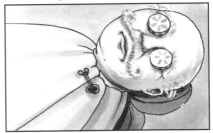

Principal Russ really relaxes.

BATHROOMS *(Continued from page 1, column 2)*
like the one at Stonehenge."

So that's what those boulders around town are all about!

How to explain the presence of Roman coins, writings and design elements in our local baths?

"Either the Romans spent time here," said Minnie O., "or they traded with the people who lived here, which would explain the foreign coins. Another possibility is that the Romans became pen pals with the early settlers of Geyser Creek. Maybe they exchanged ideas about their bathrooms, just like we did with Florence from her Bath room."

"Lost" Historical Records Found in Sting Ray's office

By Tad Poll, Investigative Reporter-in-Training

Sally Mander dishes the dirt while Sting Ray comes clean.

Historical documents allegedly lost by former town historian Liz Ard have been found in Sting Ray's office, said agents with Lily Pad's Private Investigations, Etc.

Through interviews conducted last night and this morning at the Geyser Creek County Jail, the student-run private investigation firm pieced together the bizarre crime quadrangle of Sally Mander, Delbert "Dee" Eel, Sting Ray and Liz Ard.

According to Lily and Paddy, the saga began 32 years ago, when Liz Ard discovered the secret journals and maps of Spanish explorer Ponce de León.

"Liz blabbed the secret to her sister, Sally Mander, who moved to town with her accomplice, Dee Eel, and promptly stole the maps and documents from Liz," said Lily.

Together, Mander and Eel built a new middle school on what they thought was the Fountain of Youth, believing that eternal youth and fortunes lay below.

"But when they drilled they found just water," said Paddy, "which they diverted for their greedy purposes."

As fifth graders these students also cracked that case.

"What we didn't know was that when Sting

Ray searched Sally's and Dee's offices, he found Ponce de León's journals and maps," said Paddy.

Rather than turning the documents over to the court as evidence in the case against Mander and Eel, Ray began his own covert plot to find the Fountain of Youth.

It was while searching for the Fountain of Youth that Ray discovered the treasure trove of antiquities buried in the ancient baths beneath Geyser Creek Middle School, which he began to sell online under the alias *Dasyatislata*.

In June, Ray entered into a *quid pro quo* agreement with Mander and Eel in which he agreed to secretly release them from jail if they would dig up more loot for him.

While free, Mander and Eel were able to follow their case in the *Gazette*, thanks to the newspapers in the compost heap behind school. More intriguing to the escapees, however, were the ads for The Fountainhead Salon.

"Sally and Dee became convinced that Pearl O. Ster had discovered the Fountain of Youth," said Lily. "They were determined to get it for themselves."

(See Fountain of Youth story on page 4.)

Fountain designer Florence Waters unveiled Principal Walter Russ's new management philosophy to SPA members:

The Wally Russ Management Philosophy

Write your own correspondence.

Always welcome the opinions and ideas of others.

Live bravely and take risks.

Learn the rules but don't always *live* by them. Some rules are meant to be broken.

Yell not, especially when you're angry.

Respect yourself, others and the earth, fully and equally.

Understand the connection between your mind, body and spirit.

Spend some time every day doing *nothing*! And remember:

Sanitas per aquas, or Health through Waters!

Fountain of Youth: Fact or Fiction?

By Tad Poll, Investigative Reporter-in-Training

Experts have confirmed the authenticity of Ponce de León's documents discovered in Lieut. Sting Ray's office yesterday, including the famous explorer's maps and journals in which he chronicled his search for the Fountain of Youth.

Does such a thing even exist?

"Of course it does," insisted Florence Waters. "But how silly of Ponce de León and modern-day conquistadors like Sally Mander, Dee Eel, Liz Ard and Sting Ray to think that there was only *one* Fountain of Youth."

According to Waters, fountains of youth are all around us.

"Just look at Pearl's beauty shop," she said. Pearl O. Ster confirmed that she never felt younger than this summer, when she stopped working so hard and started spending more time simply relaxing.

"Seemed like the less I did, the younger I got," Ster said. "Some days I didn't do anything but soak my head in a shampoo tub and read magazines."

Waters said the ancient baths discovered beneath Geyser Creek Middle School are a perfect example of how ancient civilizations remained youthful by managing stress.

"Our ancestors knew that spending time relaxing near water is essential for maintaining good health," Waters said. "The word *spa* comes from the Latin phrase *sanitas per aquas,* which means 'health through waters.' "

According to Waters, a fountain of youth is any place near water where people can go to celebrate the art of doing nothing.

"And *that's* the secret to eternal youth," Waters said. "Well, that and being truthful. Have you ever noticed that people who tell lies age so quickly and quite unattractively? Maybe telling the truth is another fountain of youth."

STILL OPEN FOR BUSINESS

Trap Returns from NEWS Conference to Big News

By Annette Trap, Editor

Trap promotes Poll to full-fledged reporter.

I returned from the National Editors Workshop Seminar (NEWS) this afternoon to quite a surprise.

Instead of following my directions and reporting the arrest of Florence Waters, Tad Poll, my investigative reporter-in-training, broke a major news story.

Not only that, Tad single-handedly wrote and photographed all the stories (with the exception of the Idea Box and this short article) for *two* editions of the *Gazette,* which he laid out, put to bed *and* delivered to all of our home subscribers.

Hats off to Tad "Scoop" Poll, who can remove the "in-training" from his byline. Your next assignment, Tad, is to take some time off! *[Thanks, Ms. Trap. It was a lot of work, but it was really fun, too. If possible, I'd love to keep volunteering for the Gazette. –T. P.]*

IDEA BOX

Here's the best idea submitted to the idea box today (if I do say so myself).

As compiled by Shelly, Mayor I. B. Newt's summer intern

MY IDEA IS: Hey, everybody! It's so obvious, isn't it? We'll turn Geyser Creek into a spa resort! Who wouldn't want to come here and visit our geyser, volcano, ancient baths, prehistoric wall drawings and stone calendar? We'll be the nation's first *gee*ological destination! —Shelly

SOCIETY OF PRINCIPALS AND ADMINISTRATORS

Making the World Safe for Bureaucracy

101 Maple Leaf Plaza   Washington, D.C.

Jack Oozy
President

OVERNIGHT MAIL

September 1

Walter Russ
Principal
Geyser Creek Middle School
Geyser Creek, Missouri

Dear Mr. Russ,

This will confirm that yesterday's SPA conference in Geyser Creek was the best ever.

I am urging *all* school principals and administrators to adopt the Wally Russ Management Philosophy as standard operating procedure.

To implement this initiative, I am asking that you take a one-semester sabbatical from your duties as principal of Geyser Creek Middle School so that you can lead workshops around the country devoted to your management philosophy, including *sanitas per aquas*.

I'd like you to begin immediately. Please let me know your availability.

Sincerely,

Jack Oozy

Jack Oozy
President

GEYSER CREEK MIDDLE SCHOOL
From the Principal's Desk
$Sanitas\ per\ aquas.$

(Health through waters.)

Mr. Walter Russ
Principal

September 2

Mr. Jack Oozy
President
Society of Principals and Administrators
101 Maple Leaf Plaza
Washington, D.C.

Dear Mr. Oozy,

I am forwarding your letter to my summer intern, Gil, who deserves much of the credit for the success of the SPA conference. I have learned that a principal is only as successful as the people around him or her. (Don't know how I would've survived this summer without you, Gil.)

I would be honored to share my new management philosophy with other principals—if I can find someone to take my place. I am contacting my substitute of choice and will be in touch shortly.

Sincerely,

Walter Russ

cc: Gil
        Mr. Sam N.

Lily Pad's

Private Investigations, Etc.

c/o **Geyser Creek** Middle School

Geyser Creek, Missouri

Founders and Agents: Lily and Paddy
His, Hers, and Theirs-torical Research: Minnie O.
Investigative Research: Tad Poll
Director of Ideas: Shelly
Administration: Gil

September 2

Florence Waters
Our Accomplice in FUN
Flowing Waters Fountains, Etc.
Watertown, California

Dear Florence,

Will you ever forget the look on Wally's face when he saw the Jawlseedat Mountain erupt?

Or when we told him we'd discovered a mole in the Geyser Creek sheriff's office . . .

And ancient bathrooms buried under our basement bathrooms?

The funny thing is, when we told Wally all we've learned regarding the bathrooms, he said: "Henceforth we should all spend an hour or two every day relaxing in our bathrooms." Then he said he had to go—

— because he had an appointment for a pedicure and foot massage. Can you believe it?!

Well, thanks for showing Wally—and us—the importance of reading, writing, arithmetic, *and* relaxation. And *geology* and Latin, too!

But most of all, thanks for being our *magna amicus*. That's Latin for "GREAT FRIEND"!

From our bathroom to yours,

Tad   *Shelly*   Minnie O.   Lily   Paddy   Gil

P.S. *Sanitas per (Florence) Waters!*

134

September 2

Florence Waters
Friend and Fount of Endless In*spara*tion
Flowing Waters Fountains, Etc.
Watertown, California

Dear Florence,

Once again, you left town before we had a chance to thank you properly.

And before we could tell you the big news. Florence, I'm not sick at all. I'm pregnant! Angel is, too! We're both due in February.

(As I say, I'm always the last to know.)

Florence, have you heard that Wally will be gone next semester? Guess who he's asked to fill in for him? Yep, my wonderful, adorable, brilliant husband!

Meanwhile, my beautiful, wonderful (especially now that she's over her morning sickness) bride and I were wondering: Is there any chance you might be willing to take over my class for the fall semester? I know it's a lot to ask. Please think about it and let us know.

Fondly,

Sam Goldie and our baby-to-be

P.S. Thanks for encouraging me to draw Goldie a bath. Here's a bath drawing for *you.*

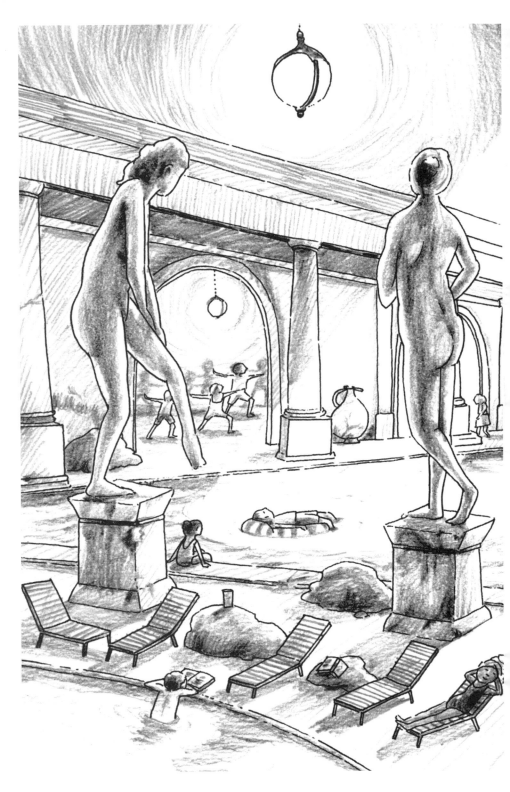

FLOWING WATERS FOUNTAINS, ETC.

Watertown, California

September 5
Labor Day!

The Bathing Beauties at
Geyser Creek Middle School
Geyser Creek, Missouri

Dear Friends,

I so enjoyed seeing you all again last week. What amazing luck to discover an ancient spa beneath your school just in time for the SPA conference!

I'm glad you share my love of baths. And to think you discovered what Sally Mander, Dee Eel, Liz Ard, Sting Ray, and Ponce de León never found: the Fountain of Youth. It's true, you know: Relaxing in or near water will keep you young forever. Look at me!

Well, I'd better run. I'm teaching a water ballet class in my pool in ten minutes.

Happy Labor Day. I hope you're celebrating by *not* laboring— unless, of course, it's a labor of love.

Ex animo (that's Latin for "from the heart"),

Florence

P.S. Congratulations to Sam and Goldie! And to Angelo and Angel! But me—a substitute teacher? Let me think about it, okay?

P.P.S. to Lily and Paddy: I'm still a little miffed at Hugh for believing Sting instead of you. I told him a *mea culpa** would not be inappropriate.

*That's Latin for "my fault."

138

(i)NTERPOL
International Criminal Police Organization
Lyon, France

Hugh Dunnit
Director of Investigations

6 September

Lily Pad's Private Investigations, Etc.
c/o Geyser Creek Middle School
Geyser Creek, Missouri USA

Lily and Paddy:

Thank you for your help in stinging Sting Ray. And please
forgive me for holding your youth against you. I should have
known better. Florence was exactly your age when she began
volunteering at Interpol.

I hope I can count on your help in future cases. And, of
course, there's no need to send your CVs. Your work on this
case speaks for itself. Like Florence, you are truly *special*
agents.

Sincerely,

Hugh Dunnit
Hugh Dunnit

P.S. It seems your sheriff could also use your assistance. I'm
enclosing a pair of two-way radios for this purpose.

Citizens Band Radio

Transcript

Date: September 9   Time: 1320

Hi, Sheriff Mack Rell! Lily and Paddy here. Now that Sting's in jail, you might be a little short-handed. We're here to help if you need us. We also want to tell you that Angel's back at Cafe Florence. She's invented a new donut inspired by you! Over and out.

((◖ ALL POINTS BULLETIN ◗))

Geyser Creek County Sheriff's Office

Date: September 9   **Time:** 1345

Sheriff Mack Rell here saying howdy girls and thanks for the good news. How 'bout letting me buy you and your associates at Lily Pad's Private Investigations, Etc., a dozen or so of those new donuts in appreciation for all your work on the case? Sound good? Oh, Mayor Newt just called. He wants to do one of those special proclamation thingies at Cafe Florence. We'll be there in a jiffy. Thanks and bye-bye. I mean, over and out.

OFFICIAL PROCLAMATION

HIS HONOR
MAYOR I. B. NEWT

WHEREAS, it has recently been discovered that the Jawlseedat Mountain is, in fact, a volcano, and

WHEREAS, our geyser here in Geyser Creek has never been officially named, and

WHEREAS, we now have proof positive that relaxing every day in or near water helps keep a person young;

I hereby proclaim that:

● The Jawlseedat Mountain will henceforth be called Mt. Jawlseedat;

● Our geyser will henceforth be called Young Hopeful (to avoid confusion with Old Faithful);

● All residents of Geyser Creek will be encouraged to spend time every day relaxing in or near water;

● Anyone who is seen working too hard will be escorted by me or Sheriff Mack Rell to the new Geyser Creek Baths & Spa for one hour of mandatory loafing around and/or goofing off;

● Chef Angelo and Angel Fisch are required by law to stay married and keep Cafe Florence open because some of us nearly starved to death this summer.

I would also like to add a special commendation for those terrific kids at Geyser Creek Middle School who spent their summer volunteering for me and others, and who worked together to crack the case of the century last week over at Pearl's beauty shop.

Signed on this day,
September 9

I. B. Newt

Mayor of Geyser Creek, Missouri

THE GEYSER CREEK GAZETTE

Our motto: "We have a nose for news!"

Saturday, September 10   Early Edition   50 cents

School Schedule Revamped to Reflect Principal's New Philosophy

By Tad Poll, Investigative Reporter

When students return to Geyser Creek Middle School next week to begin the fall semester, they'll find a new schedule.

"Principal Russ believes in the importance of taking time off every day to relax and do nothing," said Gil, administrative assistant to Walter Russ.

Gil explained that the new school schedule will begin at 8 a.m.

"At noon we'll break for lunch," said Gil. "We invite parents and everyone in the community to join us for a delicious midday meal at Cafe Florence."

After lunch classes will adjourn for a two-hour siesta, during which time students, faculty members and everyone in the community are encouraged to spend time relaxing at the Geyser Creek Middle School fountain, located on the first floor of the school, or in the newly discovered ancient baths beneath the school basement.

Following the siesta students will spend two hours on homework or independent study.

"Principal Russ hopes everyone enjoys the new schedule," said Gil, who will serve as a liaison between the school and Principal Russ while he is in Washington, DC. (See story on page 2.)

Principal Walter Russ demonstrates his new position on administration.

Sting Ray Sentenced

By Tad Poll, Investigative Reporter

Ray and Eel share cell next to Mander and Ard.

Sting Ray was sentenced yesterday to 99 years in Geyser Creek County Jail.

At his trial Sting pled *nolo contendere*, which is Latin for "I do not wish to contend." A *nolo contendere* plea is equivalent to an admission of guilt that allows a defendant the legal option of denying the charges later.

Ray is sharing a jail cell with Delbert "Dee" Eel, next to a cell shared by Liz Ard and her sister, Sally Mander.

"I can't believe I have to share a cell and a tiny bathroom with my stupid sister," said Ard.

"It's cruel and unusual punishment," agreed Mander. "We're going to file an appeal or something."

(Continued on page 2, column 2)

Fall Semester School Schedule

8:00 a.m. to noon: morning classes

Noon to 1:00 p.m.: lunch

1:00 to 3:00 p.m.: siesta

3:00 to 5:00 p.m.: independent study

Ster to Manage Geyser Creek Baths & Spa

Stylist Ster will move shop to spa.

Pearl O. Ster, relaxed owner of the Fountainhead Salon, has been tapped to manage the new Geyser Creek Baths & Spa, located beneath Geyser Creek Middle School. "I'm just so ding-dang excited," said Ster, who will move her beauty salon to the spa.

Ster will work with Jim Nayzium, who was formerly Goldie Fisch-N.'s personal trainer. Nazyium lost his job when Goldie discovered her weight gain was due to pregnancy.

Walter Russ Leaves for Washington, DC

Florence Waters to teach fall semester—by correspondence course!

A relaxed Russ begins new job.

Geyser Creek Middle School Principal Walter Russ left yesterday for Washington, DC.

Russ will spend the fall semester working for the Society of Principals and Administrators (SPA), sharing his new management philosophy with school principals and administrators around the country.

Geyser Creek Middle School teacher Sam N. will serve as principal until Russ returns.

And who will take Mr. N.'s place? Florence Waters!

The famous fountain designer has agreed to teach Mr. N.'s students—by correspondence course.

STING RAY *(Continued from page 1, column 2)*

Judge Anne Chovey responded by ordering the women to be released every afternoon under police supervision so that they can provide free manicures to all visitors to the Geyser Creek Baths & Spa.

"They want to file something?" said Judge Chovey. "They can file nails."

"That's the funniest thing I ever heard in my life," said Ray when he heard about the judge's order.

Judge Chovey then ordered that if Ray thought the idea was so funny, he and Eel could provide free pedicures for spa visitors every day during siesta.

"Serves them right for being such heels," Chovey said.

FINIS

(That's Latin for "The End.")

COMING SOON!

Regarding the Bees

A Lesson, in Letters, on Honey, Dating, and Other Sticky Subjects

What's the buzz in Geyser Creek?

Turn the page to find out....

Can a bee be in a spelling bee?

That's what the seventh graders at Geyser Creek Middle School want to know after Florence Waters sends them a honeybee named Honey that uses its tiny body to spell words.

Waters, the famous designer, is teaching the class by correspondence course. She's supposed to be preparing the class for the annual Basic Education Evaluation (BEE). But when Florence hears about the BEEs— *They're long. They're awful. They follow kids to college!*—she vows to help her students battle these beasts. And so, off she goes to research bees and honey hunting.

Meanwhile, an even more dangerous hunt for honey is under way in the seventh-grade class as students begin the heebie-jeebie-filled search for their own sweeties.

"In a way," one beleaguered student writes to Florence, "I wish we could all go back to fifth grade, when everybody in our class was friends."

In the next installment in the Regarding the ... series, author Kate Klise and illustrator M. Sarah Klise take on the ever-sticky subjects of honey, dating, test taking, communicating, and the age-old question: How in the world do you find your honey?

(Answer: *Very* carefully!)

Author **Kate Klise** (left) and illustrator **M. Sarah Klise**
are the collaborative sisters responsible for such convo*loo*ted
comedies as *Regarding the Fountain, Regarding the Sink,*
and *Regarding the Trees*. Regarding the Klises, they grew
up sharing a bathroom in Peoria, Illinois. Kate now lives,
writes, and bathes at her home in the Missouri Ozarks.
Sarah draws both her pictures and her baths in Berkeley,
California.

To learn more about these plumb crazy Klise sisters, visit
their website at **www.kateandsarahklise.com**.

Can a bee be in a spelling bee?

That's what the seventh graders at Geyser Creek Middle School want to know after Florence Waters sends them a honeybee named Honey that uses its tiny body to spell words.

Waters, the famous designer, is teaching the class by correspondence course. She's supposed to be preparing the class for the annual Basic Education Evaluation (BEE). But when Florence hears about the BEEs— *They're long. They're awful. They follow kids to college!*—she vows to help her students battle these beasts. And so, off she goes to research bees and honey hunting.

Meanwhile, an even more dangerous hunt for honey is under way in the seventh-grade class as students begin the heebie-jeebie-filled search for their own sweeties.

"In a way," one beleaguered student writes to Florence, "I wish we could all go back to fifth grade, when everybody in our class was friends."

In the next installment in the Regarding the ... series, author Kate Klise and illustrator M. Sarah Klise take on the ever-sticky subjects of honey, dating, test taking, communicating, and the age-old question: How in the world do you find your honey?

(Answer: *Very* carefully!)

Author **Kate Klise** (left) and illustrator **M. Sarah Klise**
are the collaborative sisters responsible for such convo*loo*ted
comedies as *Regarding the Fountain, Regarding the Sink,*
and *Regarding the Trees.* Regarding the Klises, they grew
up sharing a bathroom in Peoria, Illinois. Kate now lives,
writes, and bathes at her home in the Missouri Ozarks.
Sarah draws both her pictures and her baths in Berkeley,
California.

To learn more about these plumb crazy Klise sisters, visit
their website at **www.kateandsarahklise.com**.

Spa comes from the Latin phrase _sanitas per aquas_, which means "health through waters."

Roman spas were designed for people who wanted to socialize, and for those who wanted to relax alone.

The Romans gathered in spas to debate, eat, pray, work out, and unwind with friends.